712

The Running Dream

Also by Wendelin Van Draanen

Sammy Keyes and the Hotel Thief
Sammy Keyes and the Skeleton Man
Sammy Keyes and the Sisters of Mercy
Sammy Keyes and the Runaway Elf
Sammy Keyes and the Curse of Moustache Mary
Sammy Keyes and the Hollywood Mummy
Sammy Keyes and the Search for Snake Eyes
Sammy Keyes and the Art of Deception
Sammy Keyes and the Psycho Kitty Queen
Sammy Keyes and the Dead Giveaway
Sammy Keyes and the Wild Things
Sammy Keyes and the Cold Hard Cash
Sammy Keyes and the Wedding Crasher

• • •

How I Survived Being a Girl
Flipped
Swear to Howdy
Runaway
Confessions of a Serial Kisser

WENDELIN VAN DRAANEN

The Running Dream

ALFRED A. KNOPF 🐎 NEW YORK

THIS IS A BORZOI BOOK PUBLISHED BY ALFRED A. KNOPF

Visit us on the Web! www.randomhouse.com/teens

Educators and librarians, for a variety of teaching tools, visit us at
www.randomhouse.com/teachers

Library of Congress Cataloging-in-Publication Data
Van Draanen, Wendelin.
The running dream / Wendelin Van Draanen. — 1st ed.
p. cm.
Summary: When a school bus accident leaves sixteen-year-old Jessica an amputee, she returns to school with a prosthetic limb and her track team finds a wonderful way to help rekindle her dream of running again.
ISBN 978-0-375-86667-8 (trade) — ISBN 978-0-375-96667-5 (lib. bdg.)
— ISBN 978-0-375-89679-8 (ebook)
[1. Running—Fiction. 2. Amputees—Fiction. 3. Prosthesis—Fiction.
4. People with disabilities—Fiction. 5. High schools—Fiction. 6. Schools—Fiction.] I. Title.
PZ7.V2857Rv 2011
[Fic]—dc22
2010007072

The text of this book is set in 12-point Goudy.

Printed in the United States of America
January 2011
10 9 8 7 6 5

First Edition

The Running Dream

contents

PART I

Finish Line

chapter 1

My life is over.

Behind the morphine dreams is the nightmare of reality.

A reality I can't face.

I cry myself back to sleep, wishing, pleading, praying that I'll wake up from this, but the same nightmare always awaits me.

"Shhh," my mother whispers. "It'll be okay." But her eyes are swollen and red, and I know she doesn't believe what she's saying.

My father—now that's a different story. He doesn't even try to lie to me. What's the use? He knows what this means.

My hopes, my dreams, my life . . . it's over.

The only one who seems unfazed is Dr. Wells. "Hello there, Jessica!" he says. I don't know if it's day or night. The second day or the first. "How are you feeling?"

I just stare at him. What am I supposed to say, Fine?

He inspects my chart. "So let's have a look, shall we?"

He pulls the covers off my lap, and I find myself face to face with the truth.

My right leg has no foot.

No ankle.

No shin.

It's just my thigh, my knee, and a stump wrapped in a mountain of gauze.

My eyes flood with tears as Dr. Wells removes the bandages and inspects his handiwork. I turn away, only to see my mother fighting back tears of her own. "It'll be okay," she tells me, holding tight to my hand. "We'll get through this."

Dr. Wells is maddeningly cheerful. "This looks excellent, Jessica. Nice vascular flow, good color . . . you're already healing beautifully."

I glance at the monstrosity below my knee.

It's red and bulging at the end. Fat staples run around my stump like a big ugly zipper, and the skin is stained dirty yellow.

"How's the pain?" he asks. "Are you managing okay?"

I wipe away my tears and nod, because the pain in my leg is nothing compared to the one in my heart.

None of their meds will make that one go away.

He goes on, cheerfully. "I'll order a shrinker sock to control the swelling. Your residual limb will be very tender for a while, and applying the shrinker sock may be uncomfortable at first, but it's important to get you into one. Reducing the swelling and shaping your limb is the first step in your rehabilitation." A nurse appears to re-bandage me as he makes notes in my chart and says, "A prosthetist will be in later today to apply it."

Tears continue to run down my face.

I don't seem to have the strength to hold them back.

Dr. Wells softens. "The surgery went beautifully, Jessica." He says this like he's trying to soothe away reality. "And considering everything, you're actually very lucky. You're alive, and you still have your knee, which makes a huge difference in your future mobility. BK amputees have it much easier than AK amputees."

"BK? AK?" my mom asks.

"I'm sorry," he says, turning to my mother. "Below knee. Above knee. In the world of prosthetic legs, it's a critical difference." He prepares to leave. "There will obviously be an adjustment period, but Jessica is young and fit, and I have full confidence that she will return to a completely normal life."

My mother nods, but she seems dazed. Like she's wishing my father was there to help her absorb what's being said.

Dr. Wells flashes a final smile at me. "Focus on the positive, Jessica. We'll have you up and walking again in short order."

This from the man who sawed off my leg.

He whooshes from the room, leaving a dark, heavy cloud of the unspoken behind.

My mother smiles and coos reassuringly, but she knows what I'm thinking.

What does it matter?

I'll never run again.

chapter 2

I AM A RUNNER.

That's what I do.

That's who I am.

Running is all I know, or want, or care about.

It was a race around the soccer field in third grade that swept me into a real love of running.

Breathing the sweet smell of spring grass.

Sailing over dots of blooming clover.

Beating all the boys.

After that, I couldn't stop. I ran everywhere. Raced everyone. I loved the wind across my cheeks, through my hair.

Running aired out my soul.

It made me feel *alive*.

And now?

I'm stuck in this bed, knowing I'll never run again.

chapter 3

THE PROSTHETIST IS STOCKY and bald, and he tells me to call him Hank. He tries to talk to me about a fake leg, but I make him stop.

I just can't listen to this.

He gets the nurse to put a new bandage on my leg. One that's thinner. With less gauze.

I'm cold.

The room's cold.

Everything feels cold.

I want to cover up, but Hank is getting ready to put on the shrinker sock. It's like a long, toeless tube sock. He pulls it through a short length of wide PVC pipe, then folds the top part of the sock back over the pipe. I don't understand what he's going to do with it, and I don't care.

Until he slips the pipe over my stump.

"Oh!" I gasp as pressure and pain shoot up my leg.

"I'm sorry," Hank says, transferring the sock from the pipe onto my leg as he pulls the pipe off. "We're almost done."

Half the tube sock is now dangling from my stump. Hank slides a small ring up the dangling end, then stretches out the rest of the sock and doubles it up over the ring and over my stump.

There's pressure. Throbbing. But Hank assures me it'll feel better soon. "The area is swollen," he tells me. "Pooling with blood. The shrinker sock will help reduce the swelling and speed your recovery. Once the wound is healed and the volume of your leg is reduced, we can fit you with a preparatory prosthesis."

"How long will that take?" my mother asks. Her voice starts out shaky, but she tries to steady it.

Hank whips out a soft tape measure and circles the end of my stump. "That's hard to say."

His mind seems to wander, so my mom asks, "Well, in a typical situation?"

Hank takes a deep breath. "Typical is a person in poor health. Someone with circulatory problems. Someone who's old, overweight, or suffering from diabetes." He glances at me. "A case like Jessica's will not have the same timeline. Her recovery will be much quicker."

"So what is *their* expected recovery time?" my mother asks, and she's sounding testy.

"We usually don't fit them with a preparatory prosthesis for about six months."

"Six months?" my mother gasps.

"But Jessica could have hers in a fraction of that time. It all depends on her healing and how soon she can tolerate it."

They talk some more, but I stop listening.

What does it matter how long it takes?

I'll never recover.

I can't see how I'll ever even adjust.

chapter 4

I CLOSE MY EYES and drift off.

I see the race.

Vanessa Steele's in lane five, stretching out. Her long nails painted deep red, her racing glasses flashing back the late-morning sun.

I remember thinking that Vanessa has been good for me. Her superior attitude, her mind games, her domination of the 400-meter.

It's been good for me.

Vanessa glances over her shoulder, waiting for me to get into my blocks before she gets down in hers.

It's part of her game. She likes to be the last one standing.

This time I don't mind. I'm through being sucked into her psych-out.

I feel calm.

Confident.

Kyro has been helping me focus. He's been building me up mentally and physically, coaching me for this moment.

I give Vanessa a little smile and nod from my position in lane four. She's in red and yellow—Langston High's colors.

I'm in Liberty High's blue and gold. Even my colors feel light—like the sun and the sky floating above me.

I'm down in the blocks now, ready to fly.

Vanessa makes her final adjustments, then holds steady.

The gun goes off and all runners shoot forward. It's a fury of steps, spikes against track. They thunder all around me but somehow sound miles away.

By the first bend we find our stride. My kick is good. Strong and long.

Whoosh, whoosh, whoosh, whoosh!

My arms are pumping, but they're smooth, almost relaxed.

Whoosh, whoosh, whoosh, whoosh!

My breathing's open, flowing, and I barely feel my feet touching down.

Whoosh, whoosh, whoosh, whoosh!

Suddenly I'm floating.

Flying.

Soaring around the track.

The thunder fades behind me, and the staggered start has me at a mental advantage—I can see Vanessa, but she can only feel me behind her, moving in.

At the 200-meter mark the field has widened.

All except for Vanessa and me.

We've tightened.

We crest at the 300, then face Rigor Mortis Bend.

Vanessa knows I'm here.

On her tail.

We're down to grit and guts, so I dig in.

Dig deep.

She does the same.

We battle along the straightaway, my legs burning, aching, empty. Shoulder to shoulder, I force one last push and duck over the finish line in front of her.

"Fifty-five flat!" Kyro shouts. "Fifty-five flat!"

It's a new personal best for me.

A new record for the league.

It's also the last race of my life.

My finish line.

chapter 5

Nurses come in and out. Conversations happen around me. Whispers, like a heavy fog, hang on in my mind.

But then there's my father's voice.

And Dr. Wells's.

Outside my room their words drift in through the crack in the doorway.

My father asks about things he's researched online. Rigid removable dressings. Speedier recoveries. I-pops. He sounds like a doctor.

Dr. Wells's replies revolve around small-town practicalities, insurance allowances, and the tried-and-true methods employed by Mercy Hospital.

Dad comes in and checks on me, and although he pretends to be upbeat, he's irked. He likes to fix things. Now.

He checks out the stump protector that's been put on over the shrinker sock. It holds my leg straight and keeps me from bumping the wound. He seems pleased with it and throws around phrases like "controlling edema" and "preventing knee flexion contracture."

He sounds like he knows what he's talking about.
But really he's a self-employed handyman.
And I'm not something he can fix.

chapter 6

THE CALL LIGHT'S BEEN ON for fifteen minutes and I'm just sick of waiting.

I'm sick of bedpans.

"Hand me the crutches," I growl at my mother.

She's unsure. I haven't done so well with the physical therapist.

"Hand them to me!"

She does, and I swing my legs over the edge of the bed. Carefully. Slowly. It takes a little doing, but I stand, supported by the crutches.

I'm already panting.

My mother pushes along my IV stand as I hobble toward the bathroom. "You're doing great," she says, but she's wrong. I'm dizzy. Shaking.

"Maybe I should get the nurse?" she asks as I come to a halt, exhausted from the effort.

I shake my head, angry that this is so hard.

"You're doing great," my mom repeats as I start up again. "I'm so proud of you!"

My hands death-grip the crutches and I hobble forward. A few days ago I ran a fifty-five flat in the 400-meter.

Today I'm taking five minutes to go twenty feet.

When I finally get to the bathroom, I see myself in the mirror.

Matted hair.

Puffy eyes.

Chapped lips.

I move on, then pass the crutches off to my mother, grab the support bar, and begin to lower myself onto the toilet.

But I'm weak, and my good leg gives way.

My mother gasps as I fall onto the seat with a painful thump, and then fusses as I pee all over my gown.

"It's okay!" she says as I bawl into my hands. "It was your first try. What do you expect?" She turns and calls, "Nurse? Nurse!" then tries again to soothe me. "It will get easier. Things *will* get better." But in her eyes I can see fear.

Fear that her words are lies.

Lies, lies, lies.

"Nurse!" she calls again. Louder. More desperately.

This time one appears. "Oh my," she says when she's sized up the situation. "Do we need a new gown?"

It takes the three of us ten minutes to wash and re-dress me.

Another five for me to hobble back to bed.

They help me under the covers, and after I'm tucked safely inside, my mother brushes back my hair and kisses my forehead.

I manage a weak smile, then close my eyes, destroyed.

chapter 7

Rigor Mortis Bend.

It's a place in the 400-meter race where every cell of your body locks up.

Your lungs ache for air.

Your quads turn to cement.

Your arms pump desperately, but they're stiff and feel like lead.

Rigor Mortis Bend is the last turn of any track, and at Liberty High you're greeted with a headwind.

The finish line comes into view and you will yourself toward it, but the wind pushes you back, your body begs you to give up, and the whole world seems to grind into slow motion.

Your determination is all that's left.

It forces your muscles to fire.

Forces you to stay in the race.

Forces you to survive the pain of this moment.

Your teammates scream for you to push.

Push! Push! Push!

You can do it!

But their voices are muffled by the gasping for air, the pounding of earth, the pumping of blood, the need to collapse.

Rigor Mortis Bend.

I feel like I'm living on Rigor Mortis Bend.

chapter 8

My sense of smell seems heightened.

Sometimes it's what wakes me up.

And it's not the sickly smell of hospital.

It's flowers.

Beautiful, bursting bouquets of flowers.

I have no idea who they're from, although my mother has read me every single card. She's sniffed every rose, every carnation, and has analyzed every exotic bloom. Stargazer lilies, irises, parrot tulips, tuberoses, sweet williams, columbines, amaryllis . . .

My mother's a nut for flowers.

The helium balloons sway in the gentle air currents or stand at attention.

Get Well. They command.

They're my very own round-faced cheering squad, there in the background, peeking through the fog in my mind. *Get Well.*

But I'm not sick.

I'm crippled.

Disabled.

A gimp.

Food arrives and overpowers the fragrance of flowers.

Mashed potatoes. Gravy-covered pork, or maybe turkey. Vegetable medley.

"You've got to eat," my mother says.

I sip the juice.

"Just a few bites," she says, and I try the potatoes just to make her happy.

My stomach flinches. The smell is overwhelming.

"I'm tired," I tell her, and push the tray away. "Please. Can you get this out of here?"

She takes the tray and leaves without a word. I close my eyes and drift off, only to be awakened by her standing over me with a dish of Jell-O. "Let's try a few bites of this," she says, spooning some into my mouth.

It's cool. Refreshing.

"Thanks," I whisper. My lips are dry and chapped. I lick them, then accept another bite.

"That's my girl," she says as I take the dish from her. She smiles at me and says it again. "That's my girl."

chapter 9

THE NURSE TOLD ME IT'S WEDNESDAY.

That makes it day five.

Or four and a half, depending on how you count.

I'm off the morphine drip but still on pain meds, and my head stays cloudy.

A thin curtain separates me from the moans of my new neighbor. It smells sickly in here now. Like diarrhea and disinfectant.

My flowers are drooping and dropping petals. The balloons are sagging too, losing air. It's like they're tired of trying to cheer me up. Like they want to give up too.

There have been so many calls, but I don't want to talk.

Not to anyone.

Mom thinks I should; thinks talking to people would help me.

Dad tells them I'm not ready, then kindly but firmly hangs up.

Except when Coach Kyro calls.

Then he's more firm than kind.

He's mad at him, I think, although I'm not sure why.

I don't even want to talk to my sister. Kaylee's been in and out, but I always tell her I'm tired.

Or I just pretend to be asleep.

Mom keeps pressuring me to spend more time with her, but Kaylee's only thirteen. Still in middle school. And I know how freaked out she is to see me like this. *I'm* freaked out to see me like this, and I'm a junior in high school.

I'm supposed to be the strong one.

I've always been the strong one.

But what am I supposed to say to her? To anyone? Hey, don't worry, I'm going to be *fine*, when what I want to say is, Why me?

WHY ME?

chapter 10

THE PHYSICAL THERAPIST COMES IN and makes me get up.

Makes me crutch over to a chair.

My mother watches as he stretches out my legs and both arms, then has me use weights and resistance bands. He shows me how to use a towel to stretch and strengthen my limbs.

I don't care.

"You need to keep your body going," he tells me. "Work it as much as you can."

I'm drained. Breathless. I get back into bed and wish hard for him to go away.

He turns to my mother. "Encourage her to do these as often as she'll tolerate."

When he finally does leave, there's a timid knock on the door. And when my mom sees my best friend standing there with a big get-well teddy bear, she looks at me, then waves her in.

"You *need* this," she whispers, and on her way out she murmurs to Fiona, "A quick visit, okay? She's still very fragile."

Fragile.

Me.

Fiona smiles, and I take in the beautiful sight of her. New highlights in her already blond hair. Matching light blue hoodie and shorts. Asics on her feet.

And those legs.

Long. Tan. Smooth.

I never really realized how beautiful legs could be.

She sees me staring and tugs at the white trim of her shorts. "Oh, I'm an idiot!"

"You're fine," I manage.

"No, I'm an idiot!"

"But you brought a cool bear," I tell her, and actually grin.

She hands it over and sits in a chair. "His name's Lucas. Unless you want to name him something else. He just seems like a Lucas to me, so that's what I've been calling him. This is like the twentieth time I've been here. They always tell me I can't see you. I wore pants every time, too! I'm just . . . I'm . . ." She bursts into tears, then lunges toward me and hugs me like I've never been hugged before. "I'm so sorry, Jess. I don't know what to say. I don't know what to do. I've been so scared. I miss you so much!"

I hug her back, and the lump in my throat hurts.

Hurts hard.

"I don't know what to say either," I finally choke out. "And I don't know what to do. I'm dying in here." Tears roll down my cheeks as we look at each other. "Am I pathetic or what?"

"Pathetic is so not you!" she says with a sniff. "And you're *not* dying. You're alive!" She hugs me hard again. "Thank

God you're alive! The whole thing's horrible. Horrible, horrible, horrible!" She pulls away. "But I keep thinking if you had been Lucy and she had been you, *I* would have died!"

"Lucy?" I ask, and for a moment the air seems like glass.

And then I remember.

Finally remember.

Lucy in the seat in front of me.

The light.

The sounds.

Screaming.

Crunching.

Shattering.

My breath catches and I can feel it again.

The pain.

My foot, caught, twisted, crushed.

And then darkness.

Blissful, painless darkness.

chapter 11

"ARE YOU OKAY? Jessica! Hey! Hey, look at me!"

Fiona's voice brings me back.

"What happened to Lucy?" I choke out, but my gut's way ahead of her answer.

"You don't know?" Fiona gasps. "Oh man." She backs away. "I'm an idiot. I thought for sure you knew."

"She died?"

Fiona nods. Blinks. "She didn't suffer," she blurts out. "She hit her head and was just . . . gone."

The whole room starts spinning.

Lucy.

So sweet. Her first year running. Joined the team to make friends. I brace myself. "Who else?"

"That's it. The rest of us are just cut and bruised and scarred for life."

She's serious, and for a moment I forget about my leg. "My father said the guy who hit us was killed."

"And good riddance to that loser!" she says.

"Was he . . . drunk?"

"He might as well have been! He was hauling a load of wrecked cars to a junkyard with bad brakes! He missed a turn, went off the side of the road, barreled down the embankment, and smashed into us. Talk about irresponsible. He torpedoed a school bus!"

Torpedoed.

That word was exactly right.

Fiona eyes the covers. "So . . . do I get to see?"

Oh, yeah.

The leg.

"You don't have to," she says. Her face crinkles. "Am I being an idiot again?"

I think about it, then flip back the covers and let her stare. When she's whiter than my sheets, I cover it back up and say, "You should see it unwrapped."

"Why couldn't they save it?" she asks, and her voice is choked. Almost inaudible.

"Smashed beyond repair," I tell her, and I feel odd.

Like I should be crying.

My mother eases into the room with a smile. "Are we doing okay?" she asks.

We're both dead quiet. Fiona starts blinking like there's too much light in the room, then says, "I . . . I guess my time's up." She gives me a long, hard hug and whispers, "You can do this."

Then she says goodbye to my mother and walks her long, tan legs out the door.

chapter 12

I'M IN AN ENDLESS BLUR of exhausted days and sleepless nights. The nurses are nice about my pain meds. It's the only way I get any sleep.

Dr. Wells visits every morning and leaves with a cheery prognosis. "You're healing beautifully, Jessica. Keep up the good work."

The physical therapist teaches me how to care for my stump.

I have to learn to clean it.

Learn to dress and protect it.

Learn to massage it and desensitize it.

Learn to not vomit at the sight of it.

I finally have a real visit with Kaylee.

I try to be brave, but it's hard.

"When can you come home?" she asks after we've dispensed with the small talk.

"I don't know if I want to," I say with a smart-alecky grin. "They wait on me hand and, uh, *foot* here. They clean up after me and give me massages. You gonna do that when I get home?"

A part of her's not sure I'm kidding, so I pull her in and whisper, "As soon as I can, okay?" Then I give her some space and ask, "How's Sherlock holding up? You walking him for me?"

"Dad is."

"Well, you get out there and do it too. He'll chew up all my shoes if he's cooped up too long." I smirk at her. "Okay, so he can have the right ones, but don't let him anywhere *near* the left ones."

She doesn't laugh, and I'm feeling dumb for trying so hard. She also doesn't ask to see my stump. She just hugs me some more and tells me she loves me, and after a game of gin rummy Mom gently informs her that it's time to go.

I wave goodbye and tell her, "Stay out of trouble! And hey! Stay out of my closet too! You cannot have my clothes, you hear me? I'm coming home, so don't even *think* about taking my stuff!"

"You were wonderful," Mom whispers after she's passed Kaylee off to Dad. "Absolutely wonderful."

"Thanks," I tell her, but my whole chest seems to collapse under the effort of that single, empty word.

Suddenly I'm wrung out.

Exhausted from the effort of pretending to be strong.

chapter 13

I do my physical therapy.

Mom makes me.

"It'll make you strong, darling."

Dad makes me.

"You don't want to spend the rest of your life in a bed, Jess. Get up."

Fiona makes me.

"I miss you! We need to get you out of here!"

The phone rings as I'm panting from a therapy session with Fiona. She snatches it up and says, "Jessica Carlisle's room, Nurse Bartlett speaking."

Her mouth stretches into a long, pink O as she turns to me. Her eyes are enormous. "One moment, please," she says in a very professional manner, then hands the phone over with the mouthpiece palmed. "It's Gavin Vance!"

I take the phone from her. "Hello?"

"Jessica? It's Gavin."

Something about hearing his voice stuns me silent.

I've wished for this call for almost two years.

"Uh . . . Gavin Vance?" he says, and I imagine him wondering how there could possibly be any confusion. After all, he *is* the mayor's son.

"Oh, hey," I say back.

"Uh . . . I just wanted to say . . . you know . . . I hope you're . . . you know . . ." His voice trails off.

"Back on my feet soon?" I ask.

He laughs. It's a nervous laugh, mixed with relief.

"I know," I tell him. "What can you say, huh?"

"Yeah," he says, with another nervous laugh. "Everyone feels terrible about what happened."

"Not as bad as me," I quip.

He laughs again, and this time it's not so nervous. "Hey. I'm doing an article for the *Liberty Bell* and—"

"About the accident?"

"Right. There are a lot of rumors flying around and—"

All of a sudden my body flashes hot. "Look. I'm not up to reliving that nightmare for the school paper, okay?"

"No! I'm sorry. I'm just wondering . . . well, *everyone's* wondering when you're going to be back at school."

I'm still feeling hot.

And shaky.

"I'm not sure," I say quietly. "Not for a while." And even though this is Gavin Vance, I really want to hang up on him. So I say, "I need to get back to my physical therapy," and end the conversation.

Fiona is completely bowled over. "Gavin Vance called you!"

"A dream come true," I grumble, because really, if it took losing a leg to get him to notice me, I'd rather be ignored.

chapter 14

MY MOTHER COMES IN with a to-go bag from Angelo's.

"Lasagna?" I ask.

She beams as she opens the sack. "What else?"

It smells heavenly, and for the first time since I got rushed into Mercy Hospital, I'm hungry.

Really, truly hungry.

"Oh, thank you," I say, scooting up in bed so she can wheel the tray across my lap. It takes a few scoots because the stump is very tender. Still mad at the world.

Hospital regulations say that I have to wear a gown, so when I'm situated, my mother shakes out a napkin, tucks it in my gown collar, and fusses until everything's arranged and I'm digging in.

"Mmm," I tell her with a contented smile. "It's wonderful."

She's relieved, I know, and I'm happy to not be pretending. Angelo's lasagna is amazing on any ordinary day, but at this moment it is the best thing I have ever tasted.

I close my eyes and just savor it.

And then an excruciating pain shoots up my leg.

My eyes fly open and I scream, "Get off my leg!" Only

my mother is nowhere near my leg. She's standing right beside me.

"Something's on my leg!" I cry. "Get it off!"

"There's nothing on your leg," she says, looking from me to the covers, back to me. "Absolutely nothing!"

I'm at a slant and I can't really see what's past the hospital tray, but I know she's crazy. The pain is so real. So strong. There's something on my shin, twisting my foot!

I shove the tray aside before I remember that I don't have a shin.

Or a foot.

"Another phantom pain?" my mother asks quietly.

I nod and stare at the flat covers where my foot should be. Every time I have a phantom pain, it freaks me out. They're unpredictable. And always different. Sometimes the missing part of my leg burns. Sometimes it stabs. Sometimes it feels twisted. Sometimes it's a combination. The nerves are cut, but they're still connected to my brain.

"Do you want me to get the nurse?" my mother asks, and her glowing face has been replaced by a pale, worried one.

"No," I tell her. "It's going away."

But I'm panting.

Sweating.

Her mouth quivers uncertainly. "Are you sure?"

I nod and pull the tray back toward me. And after a minute I pretend to be hungry, but really I'm not. The pain has made me nauseous, and on the other side of the tray I can still feel my leg.

It may be gone, but that's not stopping it from insisting it's still there.

chapter 15

I HAVE THE DREAM AGAIN:

Dawn is breaking.

Sherlock's whole body is wagging as he dances in a circle by the front door.

We ease out of the house, then bound down the porch steps, turning right when we hit the street to head toward the river.

The world is quiet.

No cars.

No people.

No hustle and bustle.

Just the rhythmic padding of our feet against pavement.

Sherlock is happy beside me. His white fur seems to flow through the morning mist, and he doesn't miss a beat. I turn, he turns. I speed up, he speeds up. No leash to connect us. No commands to control him. We're bound by the joy of running.

We reach the river, and the air is heavenly. It sparkles my face, washes my lungs, fills me with a sense of fluid motion. I glide beneath the trees, transform into wind.

We breeze up to Aggery Bridge and I begin the long sprint across it. My legs and lungs burn, but I welcome the pain.

I'm stronger than pain.

Sherlock races ahead and I let him. He lives to run the bridge. Reaching two legs forward, kicking two legs back. He waits for me on the other side, wagging, panting, grateful for this stretch of freedom.

He falls in beside me as I drop back the pace and glide along the streets, back past familiar houses, back home.

On the porch again, he kisses me and pants as I tousle his ears. "Good boy!" I tell him. "You are such a good boy!"

The sun is brighter now.

Our sleepy neighborhood is stirring, waking up.

And then, with a gasp, so do I.

chapter 16

I ROLL OVER and check the clock; check the chair.

4:28 AM.

The chair's empty.

I told Mom she didn't have to stay nights anymore. That I was okay. I said it with conviction.

She wanted badly to believe me.

Almost as badly as I wanted her to.

It's easy to see from the dark circles, the haunted eyes— she needs me to be okay. "I'd switch places with you, Jessica. In a heartbeat." She said it when the doctors explained that my leg was hopeless, and I know she's thought it every day since.

She'd give up both her legs to give me back the one I lost.

There's no doubt in my mind.

But she can't, and I hate that she's been sleeping in the chair.

So she's gone and I'm alone.

I feel trapped.

Scared.

Angry.
And so I cry.
Silent tears burn, then pool in my ears.
But they don't change a thing.
I wipe my eyes and check the clock again.
4:32 AM.
It's my eighth day with no leg.
An eternity.

chapter 17

FIONA VISITS WEARING BLACK LEGGINGS and a flowing purple top.

And heels.

They're low, but still, heels.

Definitely not typical Fiona-wear.

"Were you at church?" I ask, sitting up.

She nods. Solemnly. And now I see that her eyes are rimmed red.

"Lucy's memorial service," I say with a small voice. "I forgot."

She pulls up a chair and dissolves into it. "It was awful. Well, everyone said it was moving and beautiful and perfect, but I thought it was awful. They had a huge blowup picture of her, and flowers everywhere, and people got up and told funny stories about her, and they had her ballet slippers from sixth grade on display, and her favorite scarf wrapped over the podium. I kept staring at the picture. I wanted to look somewhere else, but I kept staring at it."

I pass her Lucas the bear. She hugs him fiercely and starts sobbing. "Why did she have to die? Why, why, why?"

She's not expecting an answer, and that's good because I sure don't have one. I rest my hand on her shoulder knowing I should be grateful I'm still alive, but somehow I'm not. I know it's selfish, but I can't help thinking that Lucy is the lucky one.

For Lucy there's no pain, no rehab, no learning to live disabled.

There's no anger or self-revulsion.

For Lucy there's just resting in peace.

chapter 18

FIONA APOLOGIZES FOR CRYING, then hugs me and tells me how glad she is I'm alive.

My secret thoughts feel even more selfish.

Then she switches gears. "Oh! Oh, oh, oh!"

"What?" I ask with a laugh. Her eyes are enormous, and I know what this means:

Gossip.

"Guess who was turning to Gavin for comfort at the memorial service?"

"Turning to him for *comfort*? So it's someone who was friends with Lucy?"

"No! She totally snubbed her!"

"Okaaaay . . ." I look for clues among the ceiling tiles, hoping she'll just tell me, but Fiona's big into twenty questions and I've only asked one. "So . . . it's someone on the team?"

Her head bobbles like crazy.

"A sprinter?"

She shakes her head.

"Mid-distance? Long distance?"

Shake, shake.

"So she does field events?"

Nod.

"Long jump? High jump? Discus?"

Shake, nod, shake.

It strikes me like a bolt. "Merryl?"

"Yes!" she gasps. "Can you believe that? Merryl Abrams after a guy who's not a jock."

"Are you sure she wasn't just, you know, mourning Lucy?"

"No way. It was classic Merryl-on-the-move." She scowls. "You should have seen her hanging all over him! Like she'd die or faint or, or . . . *explode* if he didn't hold her together. I heard her say, 'I can't bear the thought of that horrible, horrible day!'" She pulls a tortured face. "Can you believe that? She wasn't even on the bus!"

Which was true. The meet was an invitational, and Merryl hadn't qualified—something that didn't bother her a bit. Everyone knows that Merryl's on the team so she can put "team participation" on her college applications next year, and track is the only sport that doesn't cut.

"Gavin's too smart to fall for that," I tell her. "And what happened to Darren?"

She shrugs. "She got tired of him? Who knows."

"But . . . *Gavin*? Talk about switching party affiliations."

Fiona snorts. "Gavin may not be a jock, but he *is* the mayor's son, and he's hot. Especially since he grew that chin scruff."

"Wait. Gavin has chin scruff?"

She nods. "It looks seriously good on him, too."

"This is really lifting my spirits," I grumble.

"I'm sorry! I'm just telling you because it's so Merryl, and so ridiculous. Like he's going to fall for her manipulations?" She takes a deep breath. "So when are you getting out of here? I am sick of school without you!"

My stomach suddenly tightens. Dad's talked about me going back to school, but I can't picture it. It scares me to think about facing all those people. Seeing everyone walking. Watching them hurry up and down steps. Knowing that after school all my friends will meet at the track to run.

I look away. "Dr. Wells says I'll go home soon, but I don't know about school. . . ." My voice drifts off pathetically, so I say, "I've been thinking that I should do some sort of home-school program."

"A home-school program? Like on the Internet? No way. No *way*. That would be, like, the *worst* thing for you!" She leans forward. "Look. I'll push you. You can do this!"

At first I think she means she'll push me to get back to school. Push me to face the world. But the pit of my stomach understands what she really means. "You'll push me . . . in a wheelchair?"

"Of course! There's no way you can cover that campus on crutches. And it's going to be a while before you get your fake leg, right? So I'll deliver you to all your classes. It'll be easy!"

Lucas has somehow wound up back with me, and I find myself hugging him, feeling totally panicked.

I've barely figured out how to use the bathroom on my own.

How will I ever manage school?

chapter 19

THE STAPLES ARE OUT. Dr. Wells says I'm his fastest-healing patient ever. "I'm proud of you, Jessica. You've done an amazing job."

I want to shout, I haven't done anything! I've just existed!

And I want to hit him.

Hard.

I want to hit him for sawing off my leg.

Hit him for being so cheerful and acting like I'm a star patient when I'm really just an angry, pathetic whiner.

Then he says the magic words.

The ones I've been longing for.

The ones I'm terrified of.

The ones I thought might never, ever come, and are now suddenly here too fast.

"You are ready to go home."

"Today?" I ask, and it's a choked sound. Somewhere between dying and gasping for life.

He nods. "Assuming you pass all your PT requirements."

He looks directly at me. "You can manage your care and cleaning; change your own shrinker?"

I nod.

"You can walk across the room on crutches, go up and down four steps, transfer from standing to sitting, and fall safely?"

These are all things the PT has been making me do. I'm still wobbly, but I can do them, so I nod.

He smiles. "Then you're going home."

I know I should thank him, but the way he says "home" throws me. I'm suddenly picturing a pair of ruby slippers. Slippers I can't click together because . . . because I can't. And even though they're just in my head . . . just something from a movie . . . they glitter in my mind, and I'm suddenly desperate to click my heels together and wake up in my own bed.

With my own dog.

And both legs.

"There's no place like home," I whisper when he's gone. "No place like home."

But there are no ruby slippers.

There is no waking up.

There's just me and my ugly, useless stump.

chapter 20

I'M DRESSED IN SWEATS with the extra material of the right leg pinned up, and I've just demonstrated "fall safety" to a physical therapist I haven't worked with before, when my mother appears.

"Are you okay?" she gasps.

"Fine," I tell her, then demonstrate "recovery" by standing up. "Just passing my final exam."

"You're coming *home*," she squeals, dancing in place. Then she grabs the parked wheelchair and practically shoves it under me, kiss-kiss-kissing the top of my head, just like she did when I was little.

"You must be Jessica's mom," the PT says with a smile.

"That I am!" she says. Like being my mom is the best thing ever.

He chuckles. "Well, I'm happy to report that your daughter has mastered all the necessary functional goals for release." He scribbles on the sheet he's been quizzing me from and says, "From now on we'll be seeing her at the rehab facility." He hands my mother a couple of brochures and a small stack of papers, and after some pleasantries to me about keeping up the good work, he's gone.

My mother packs my things as I wait in the wheelchair with Lucas the bear in my lap. But it's another hour and a half before I'm being rolled down the corridor by a nurse.

Mom's not allowed to push me.

I'm not allowed to roll myself.

I guess they want to make sure they get me out of here in one piece, and that no one rolls off with Mercy Hospital property.

Dad's waiting outside the big glass doors of the hospital's front entrance. He's holding the handles of a smaller wheelchair, one that is, apparently, all mine. "Jessica!" he says, and he looks happy, too.

"Hey, Dad," I say, and my eyes sting with tears. It's the first real smile I've seen on him in forever.

I demonstrate a flawless wheelchair transfer, and after we all say goodbye to the nurse, Dad and Mom walk me across the parking lot to Dad's van.

They're all smiles and coos until I'm standing at the open passenger door trying to figure out how to "transfer" to a seat that's up so high.

I can't swing into it. . . .

I can't exactly *hop* inside. . . .

I can't grab the frame of the van with both arms and hoist myself in. . . .

We have crutches, but I'm not sure how to use them in this situation. . . .

I'm just . . . stumped.

Mom tries to help, but she's really just in the way. Dad has collapsed the wheelchair and put it in back with Lucas the bear and the rest of my things, and after watching me agonize over how to get inside his van, he simply gathers me in his arms and hoists me onto the seat.

"We'll figure it out, sweetheart," my mom says with a reassuring pat of my hand. "We'll figure it all out." She kisses me on the cheek. "For now let's just get you home!"

She tells Dad she'll see him at the house, then goes off to her car.

Dad fires up the van and tries smiling at me, but his eyes are heavy again and I know he's thinking what I'm thinking:

There's no such thing as easy.

Not anymore.

chapter 21

My heart begins racing as Dad turns onto Harken Street.

I don't really know why.

The whole ride has been snail-paced. Careful turns, complete stops, below-limit speeds. I can't decide if he's scared of jostling me or scared of having me home.

Finally we pull up to the curb behind my mother's car. A flood of emotions comes over me as I look at our house and see snapshots in my mind:

Mud castles in the flower beds.

Hide-and-seek under the porch.

Dad taking the training wheels off my bike.

Kickball.

Hula hoops.

Running through the sprinklers.

Sherlock as a puppy, chasing his tail.

Fiona and me giggling, climbing out my window and dropping to the ground.

And then I notice the ramp—the one that goes up the left side of the porch steps.

And the guardrail made of pipe—the one attached to the right side of the porch stairs.

They're nasty scars across a cheery entrance.

I face my dad. "I can do steps, you know. I don't need a ramp." I don't mean to, but I sound angry.

"It's just temporary," he says softly. "Until you get your leg."

I grab my crutches. "In the meantime, I can use crutches or hop." I open the passenger door defiantly, then look down at the curb. *You can do this*, I tell myself. *You can do this. Down is way easier than up.*

But the curb seems miles away, and I'm suddenly gripped with fear.

Dad's already around to my side, and he seems to understand that picking me up would be the wrong move to make. "Grab the handle and the frame," he says, coaching me forward. "Do it once and you'll have it conquered."

So I give up on the crutches and I do as he says, letting him be my spotter as I swing down to earth.

"See?" he says with a smile.

Mom's rushing from the house. "You're here!" she cries, but my dad gives her the take-it-easy signal as I saddle my armpits over the crutches.

"Uh . . . ," she says as I swing toward the steps.

She's worried.

She wants me to use the wheelchair.

I ignore her concerns as I hobble forward, and I can sense my dad pulling her back.

At the steps I put both crutches in my left hand, grab the pipe rail with my right, then hop up.

One step.

I feel off balance.

Two steps.

Like I should be grabbing the rail with my left hand.

Three.

I steady myself at the top, then saddle the crutches again and move on.

To my surprise the screen door doesn't fight me as I pull it open. Dad's disconnected the automatic closer so it swings easily and stays cooperatively to the side.

I push open the front door and cross the threshold. I'm shaky from the effort. My stump is throbbing. I just want to collapse.

Then I smell something.

Onions and oregano and garlic—Mom's spaghetti sauce heating up on the stove.

I crutch forward a few steps and take a deep breath.

From behind a gate in the kitchen Sherlock lets out a happy bark.

"Hey, boy!" I call, which makes him go berserk.

I have no ruby slippers, and I won't wake up from this dream, but still.

There's no place like home.

chapter 22

KAYLEE AND HER PACK of friends blast through the door after school.

Our house has always been their hangout.

"Oh, hey!" they say, stopping in their tracks when they see me in the hallway. It's a warm day, and they're all wearing shorts.

"Hey," I say back, and put on my best smile.

"When did you get home?" Kaylee asks.

"A little while ago," I answer.

"Hi, girls!" my mom calls from the kitchen. "Come on in!"

Kaylee's friends are trying hard not to look at my leg, and I can't help looking at theirs.

None of us seem to have anything to say.

I'm a stranger.

A freak.

"Well, I need to sit down," I finally tell them, because my stump is throbbing.

I sound angry.

Annoyed.

They move aside as I crutch past them, and in a flurry of whispers they escape up the stairs to Kaylee's room.

I retreat to the family room, take my pain meds, and turn on the TV.

chapter 23

I LEARN TO HOP AROUND THE HOUSE. I stay near furniture and walls to steady myself, and although I feel like I'm lumbering and loud, it's easier than using crutches.

My bed and dresser are downstairs in the family room. Instead of sleeping in the last room on the right upstairs, I'm now in the first room on the left after you come in the front door. I'm separated from the entry hall by a half wall with white balusters.

I don't know where they moved the couches, but I do know they did a lot of heavy lifting to set this up for me, and that I should be more appreciative than I am. It's hard, though, because I feel like a stranger in my own house. I can't get to the things I want, I can't find the things I need, and I spend way too much time watching TV. The only time I feel halfway normal is when we're at the kitchen table. It's like seeing each other from the waist up helps us forget about the stump lurking beneath the surface.

I also feel like a stranger to myself.

Everything irritates me, and cheery people just make that worse.

My friends call. They come by. They bring me plants and chocolate and get-well cards. They want to *cheer . . . me . . . up.*

It isn't working.

When they're here, I'm quiet and awkward and I can't wait for them to leave.

When they're gone, I cry.

I cry, and wish they'd come back.

They won't, though, and I know it.

I probably wouldn't either.

chapter 24

I'VE BEEN PUSHING THE CLOCK on my pain meds.

Taking them early.

Slipping in an extra when I really need it.

I tell myself that tomorrow I'll feel better.

That I'll take one less rather than one extra.

But the only time I feel better is when the meds kick in.

I'm afraid of the pain without them.

Afraid of the day without them.

Then I tell my mom I need a refill, and somehow my father gets involved.

I hear them whispering.

Arguing.

I hear him make a phone call and I pray it's to the pharmacy, but I'm pretty sure it's not.

I pretend to be asleep when he comes to see me, but this doesn't stop him.

"Jessica!" he whispers hoarsely, shaking my shoulder.

"Hm?" I answer, acting groggy.

He's holding the bottle of pills. "How often do you take these?"

"Hm?" I sit up a little. "Oh. Just when I'm supposed to," I lie.

"Are you sure?"

I nod.

He studies me.

My conscience flinches, and he sees it.

"The truth," he says.

I shrug. "I've taken a couple extras. Only when I really needed to."

He studies me a long, hard time.

He studies the pill bottle a long, hard time.

He and I both know there are only two pills left, and the math is easy.

Finally he heaves a sigh and stands. "I'm sorry," he says softly. "But we're through with these."

"No, wait!" I call after him, but he leaves the room without turning back.

chapter 25

I CAN'T GET TO SLEEP.

I'm nauseous.

Shaky.

Sweaty one minute, goose-bumpy the next.

And I'm in pain.

I cry and I moan, and when my mother comes in, I beg her to talk to my dad. "Please, Mom. They cut off my leg! Doesn't he understand? It *hurts*."

She cries with me, but in the end she sides with my dad. "It's a narcotic, honey. It's very addictive. You don't want to get dependent on it."

"But you've got to give me something!"

She comes back with Tylenol.

It does nothing for the pain.

Or the sweats or chills.

I feel abandoned.

Angry.

Raw.

But way, way down inside, I know they're right.

chapter 26

I'VE BEEN OFF THE MEDS for a few days now, which I know is good, but I'm still feeling so down. Except for Fiona, the calls have stopped. And Kaylee and her friends have found a new place to hang out.

I spend a lot of time noticing how my purple paisley bedspread clashes with the oriental rug.

I spend a lot of time reliving my last race.

Wishing for my leg back.

Crying.

I long for my own room.

My own room with four full walls and a door that closes.

I'm sick of watching TV. The bookshelf is full of Mom's favorite thrillers, but I can't seem to get into any of them. I should be catching up on my homework, but it seems so overwhelming and pointless.

What do I care about simplifying rational expressions?

I try to hide it, but Mom knows I'm feeling trapped inside this wide-open room. I say no to almost anything she suggests, so it's not her fault, it's mine.

Knowing this doesn't help, though.

Yes still comes out no.

She keeps me company when she can, but she's been busy running errands for my dad, plus keeping the books and doing the billing. She's the business end of Dad's handyman service, and since Dad has an aversion to paperwork, things would be completely disorganized without her.

Tonight she sits with me before bed and sighs softly. "Is there anything I can do for you?"

I shake my head.

I can't seem to look her in the eye, and it makes me mad at myself.

She strokes my hair. "I love you, Jessica."

My chin quivers. "I love you, too, Mom."

"Maybe it would help to have Kaylee sleep down here with you? I'm sure she'd—"

"No!" I tell her. "I'll be *fine*."

I hate that it comes out angry.

She's quiet a moment, then whispers, "Things will get better. I promise you, they will."

I nod, but I still don't believe it, even though things *are* better than they were. I've been to PT twice, and back to see Dr. Wells once. Everyone's very "impressed." They all say how great I'm doing.

And I'm moving around better. My stump still hurts, especially since I've been off the meds. But this morning I noticed a real improvement when I went through the massage and desensitizing routine. The rough-towel treatment didn't seem so rough. I found I could massage harder.

So why am I so cranky?

"I'm sorry I'm being like this," I manage. "I think I'm just tired."

"Remember," she says after a moment, "every day is another day closer to getting your new leg." She kisses me on the forehead and stands. "You heard Dr. Wells today. He says you're healing very quickly."

I nod and force a smile. "I know." Then I settle in for the night while she gets the lights just right and eases out.

And I do sleep.

For about two hours.

Then at 11:04 I wake up really having to use the bathroom.

I try to ignore it, but there's no going back to sleep. So I get out of bed and hop down the hallway, but as I near the bathroom, I hear a sound.

It's soft.

Unfamiliar.

I pass the bathroom door and continue toward the kitchen.

Hop, hop, hop.

I brace myself against the entry and see my mom with her head buried in her arms, weeping at the table.

Hop, hop, hop. I lower myself into the chair next to her and about give her a heart attack.

"Jessica!" she gasps, sitting up, revealing the family photo album under her arms.

She tries to close it, but I take it from her, and for the first time in weeks I see my right leg.

My whole right leg.

Gold shorts, royal blue singlet, three medals around my neck, and two legs.

Two strong, smooth, and furiously fast legs.

She tries to pull the picture away, but I anchor it and stare at my legs. And after a full minute of staring, I close the album and shove it to the side.

I want to say *something*, but I can't find the words, and neither can she.

All we can do is wrap our arms around each other and hold on tight.

PART II

Headwind

chapter 1

SHERLOCK NUDGES ME AWAKE AT 5:45.

Just like he has every morning since I started running with him.

"No, boy," I tell him. "No."

He whimpers, licks my face, and waits, his tail sweeping across the floor.

Sherlock's bed was moved from the kitchen into the family room, and at first it was hard because he wouldn't leave my stump alone. He knew something was wrong. Different. He would sniff it, or try to get near it to check it out. Thankfully, he's over that now and just spends his time hanging out with me.

I love him so much.

He is always good, faithful company.

But at 5:45 every morning he makes me cry.

Especially when he wakes me from the running dream.

Sherlock whines softly, and my eyes begin to burn. But then I remember my mother crying at the table, and the stinging is replaced by a flush of adrenaline.

Of anger.

Not at the guy who crashed into our bus.

Not at God.

At me.

I swing my legs over the edge of the bed and give Sherlock a kiss on the muzzle. "Where's your ball, boy?"

He scrambles across the room, fetches it from his bed, and drops it in my lap.

I'm already wearing the sweatpants Mom shortened on the right side. They're quick and comfortable, and I don't have to deal with a floppy pant leg. My sweatshirt is within reach, so getting dressed is easy, and really, Sherlock deserves better than what I've been delivering.

I pull on the sweatshirt.

Slip into a shoe.

Rake my hair into a ponytail.

Sherlock spins in a circle and barks.

"Shhh!" I whisper. "Just the ball, okay?" I put the tennis ball in front of his face so he's clear about what we're doing before I let him out.

He wags and pants, and when I'm pretty sure we have an agreement, I ease open the front door and hop out after him.

He waits for me at the bottom of the porch steps.

"Good boy," I tell him, then set up to throw the ball across the front yard.

It's not a big yard, so it would help if I could go into one corner and throw to the other, but I didn't bring a crutch, and with Mom's flower beds the way they are, there's nothing I can use for support.

So I just toss the ball from beside the pipe railing and teach Sherlock to put the ball in my hand instead of at my feet.

My foot.

He has fun, and when I'm worn out, I sit on the porch step and pet him and tell him he's a good, good boy.

It's peaceful out, and for a moment I enjoy sitting with Sherlock, sharing the morning.

But then I hear something.

Something that makes my heart leap, then crash to the pit of my stomach.

I don't want to hear this.

Don't want to see it.

Still, I can't turn away.

Sherlock's ears perk. He stops panting and stares out at the sidewalk too, so I hold on to his collar, afraid that he'll bolt off the porch.

And then there he is.

In light gray sweats.

Lost in his own rhythmic world.

A runner.

chapter 2

I BUMP INTO KAYLEE on my way back inside.

She barely grunts hello.

"Good morning to you too," I tell her as she goes past me again with a pair of jeans out of the dryer.

She stops in her tracks and turns to face me. "You're criticizing *me* for being grumpy?"

"Well, you just blast by me like I'm not even here."

"So . . . I'm supposed to be a mind reader?"

"What's *that* supposed to mean?"

She puts a hand on her hip. "Look, you act like you hate everyone and everything, you never talk. . . . What do you want from me?"

I look from side to side. "Uh . . . a little civility?"

"Nice idea," she says, pounding up the stairs. "Why don't you try it?"

I stand there for a good five minutes, stunned.

I want to shout, Why don't you try losing a leg and see what it's like.

I want to chase her up the stairs and yell at her for being bratty and unfeeling and . . . and just *wrong*.

Instead, I go back to bed and hug Lucas the bear, and when Mom leaves to take Kaylee to school, I pretend to be asleep.

When they're gone, I'm relieved. Dad's already left for a job, so I have the house to myself.

Me, myself, and my thoughts.

At first I'm glad to be alone. I don't have to pretend to be fine.

But I can't seem to get Kaylee's words out of my head.

Soon I feel anchored to my bed.

Caged in this wide-open room.

The phone rings, and when I check caller ID, I see that it's Fiona's cell. I almost don't answer, but at the last minute I punch talk. "Are you ready?" she asks. "I'm on my way over to pick you up."

She says the same thing every morning.

"No," I answer.

Just like every morning.

"C'mon, Jessica," she says with a sigh. "You can't put it off forever."

"Watch me," I grumble.

There's just the hum of traffic for a minute; then she says, "Do your parents realize how depressed you are?"

I'm quiet.

Crippled, depressed, what's the difference?

"Look, you need to get out of there. We're on half day today, so get ready, 'cause I'm coming over after school. I don't care what you say, you're getting in my car and we're going out for lunch. I'll take you to Angelo's."

"I can't," I tell her. "I'm a mess."

"Yeah, you're a mess, and we're gonna fix that. Expect me. I'll be there at around one."

"No, I mean—"

She hangs up and I'm left staring at the phone.

How can she possibly expect me to go out?

How can she expect me to deal with . . . with any of it?

First Kaylee and now Fiona?

Why don't they *get* it?

Besides, I couldn't go out even if I wanted to. I haven't had a real shower since the morning of the wreck. They tried once in the hospital, but that was more awkward than effective. And now that I'm home, I've been getting by with haphazard sponge baths, but my hair has only been washed once.

The only part of me that gets daily attention is my stump.

Massage, desensitize, clean, dry, dress.

Twice a day.

Every day.

The rest of me feels matted and mangy and . . . gross.

Yesterday Mom offered to wash my hair in the sink again, but I told her, "Maybe tomorrow." And besides the obvious slipping hazards of a one-legged shower, there doesn't happen to be a shower downstairs. Just a half bathroom—a toilet and a sink.

Fiona knows all this, so how can she expect me to go out? I know she means well, but she obviously doesn't understand what I'm going through.

So I'm a little mad. A little in a state of disbelief. And between Kaylee's snippy comments and Fiona's insisting I go to Angelo's, I get agitated and start hopping around.

I hop out of my wide-open room.

Hop over to the kitchen.

Hop all over the place.

It's as close to pacing as I can come.

Finally I find myself at the base of the stairs.

I stare up the long flight of steps.

I count the treads.

Fourteen, including the top landing.

Fourteen hard hops up.

I'm not sure I can do it. I'm not sure I should even try. It seems an ominous stretch, and I'm already tired from all my senseless hopping around.

But up those ominous fourteen steps is a shower.

A hot, massaging shower.

I think about getting a crutch, but I'd have to hop clear back to the family room for that, so I grab the handrail with both hands instead.

One hop.

Two hops.

Three.

I rest, looking up at eleven more steps, then take a deep breath.

Four hops.

Five hops.

Six.

My arms are doing a lot of the work, pulling me up as I hop. I'm panting, so I take a minute to rest, telling myself I'm almost halfway. Then I press on.

Seven steps.

Eight.

My good leg is shaking, and I feel a little dizzy, so I turn around and sit.

I'm past halfway, I tell myself. *Almost there.*

And then I discover something wonderful. By sitting down I've gained two steps! My foot is on step eight, but I'm sitting on step ten!

I put my hands down on the tread behind me, raise my foot to step nine, and push myself up backward.

I'm sitting on eleven!

I push up to twelve.

To thirteen!

My right thigh is burning from holding up my stump as I push one more time. Then I grab the handrail, hoist myself up, and take a final hop.

I look down at the run of stairs and feel an overwhelming sense of triumph.

I'm upstairs.

chapter 3

OUR SHOWER'S A COMBINATION shower-bathtub with sliding glass doors, so I can't just push aside a door and hop in. I have to get myself over the side of the tub.

I know from my experience in the hospital that it helps to have some sort of seat when I shower, so I take a little collapsible step stool that's stored behind the bathroom door and place it inside the tub, opened up. It's got rubber feet and rubber-coated steps, so it seems like it'll be secure enough, and even though the rest of the step stool is metal, I don't think Mom will mind me exposing it to rusting hazards.

After it's in place, I get everything ready. Then I stand outside the shower and put my hands here, there, all over the place.

I can't figure out how to get over this hurdle, and it makes me mad. The opening's not wide enough for me to sit on the curb and swing in. . . . I can't step over or hop over. . . .

How can this be so hard?

I find myself thinking, Why couldn't I have lost an arm instead?

If I'd lost an arm, this wouldn't be a problem—I could step right over this curb!

If I'd lost an arm, I could run circles in the shower.

I could run up and down stairs.

I could *run*.

It's useless to think this, though, so finally I grab the overhead door brace with my hands facing each other, one beside the other.

I swing my stump over the side of the tub and stand straddling the curb, trying to figure out the next step of this obstacle course.

After a few false starts, I finally use my arms to help me hop up onto the curb. The door guide is sharp against my foot, but I manage to pivot on it, then hop down into the tub.

I sit on the step stool, feeling a mixture of triumph and frustration, but when the water rains down on me, I'm washed all over with relief.

It feels so nice to just sit here.

I could sit like this all day.

Eventually I pick up the soap, and as I'm sudsing the washcloth, it crosses my mind that it would be hard to soap up with just one hand.

I try it, and it is.

It's very . . . awkward.

I start paying attention to all my movements. How one arm complements the other. And I start thinking about everything I do with two hands. Driving. Golfing. Keyboarding. Even writing really takes two hands. The pen's held in one; the paper's anchored with the other.

My mind wanders all over everyday things.

Opening a water bottle.

Getting dressed.

Making a sandwich.

Washing dishes.

I imagine life with only one hand and realize that it would be hard. In a different way, but still hard.

I squeeze shampoo into my left hand, then put down the bottle with my right.

I rub my hands together, spreading out the soap.

And as I massage both sides of my head, I'm thankful for my hands.

Thankful to have both of them.

chapter 4

MOM FREAKS OUT when she comes home.

I don't know this, because I'm rinsing my hair thinking about arms and legs and if I had a *choice* about which limb I had to give up what I would choose.

"Jessica!" she gasps when she finds me. I turn off the water as she rushes over to the tub. She's got a phone with her and says "She's in the shower" into it, then clicks off. "Did Fiona help you?" she asks.

I do a mock look-around. "Do you see Fiona anywhere?"

"You should not have come up here by yourself!" She's looking very stern. "What if you had—"

"I'm fine," I tell her, and stretch way out to snag the towel. "And clean." I give her a smile, and I feel absurdly proud of myself.

After I tousle my hair with the towel, I dry the rest of me and stand, wrapping the towel snuggly around me. Then I grab the top brace of the doorframe and shoo my mother back.

The door guide hurts again as I hop onto the tub wall, but I'm showing off now so I act like it's no big deal.

"Wow," she says when I'm standing on the other side. She's blinking at me.

It's like she's just discovered her daughter is Wonder Woman, and for a moment I feel like I am.

"How did you get upstairs?" she asks.

I tell her about my little adventure and assure her that it was safe and that I was never in danger of tumbling to my death. And I'm convincing her that my little sit-and-scoot method will be even easier going downstairs than it was coming up when I realize that my dresser's in the family room and I have no clean clothes with me.

Scooting downstairs in nothing but a towel seems like a very bad idea!

"I'll get them!" Mom offers in an overly hyper way, and she's already speed-dialing my dad as she exits the bathroom.

"Hey!" I call, hopping over and leaning out into the hallway. "No sweats, okay? I'm going out to lunch with Fiona."

"What?" She stops in her tracks and whispers to my dad, "She's going out to lunch with Fiona!"

I smile and hop back into the bathroom wondering when I decided that, and how in the world I can be feeling this good.

chapter 5

FIONA SHOWS UP a little before one o'clock. Mom's anxious because I want to take the crutches, not the wheelchair.

"What if you fall?" she asks.

Her lack of confidence annoys me. "I know how to fall, Mom. They taught me, remember?"

"But what if you *really* fall? What if—"

"Stop it! I'll be fine."

She bites back her worry and watches from the family-room window as I hop, swing, and hobble out to the curb and into Fiona's hand-me-down Subaru Outback.

"Phew," I say when I'm situated inside.

Fiona puts the key in the ignition but doesn't start the car. "We're really going out to lunch," she says, smiling at me like she can't quite believe I'm finally back in her passenger seat. "And you look great! What did you do to your hair? It's so shiny!"

I laugh. "I washed it."

She laughs too, and turns the key. "That's all?"

"Yup. I guess it's happy with me, huh?"

She pulls away from the curb. "More like ecstatic."

I roll down the window and wave at my mom, who's still watching from inside. She waves back, but even from the curb I can feel her worry, and I suddenly realize that it has nothing to do with the wheelchair or with me falling.

The last time Fiona drove me away in her Subaru, it took me more than a week to come home.

And not all of me made it.

"Can I borrow your phone?" I ask Fiona.

Mine was a casualty of the wreck.

She hands it over, and I dial the house.

"I'm fine," I tell my mother when she picks up. "Don't worry, okay? You keep telling me I should get up and out, and now I am, so you should be happy."

"I am," she says, but her voice is choked.

"Mom," I say softly, "you want me to do this."

"I know I do," she says, and she's trying hard not to, but I can tell she's crying.

"I'll call you from Angelo's, okay?"

"Thanks," she says, then gives me a cheery "Have fun, all right?"

"I don't know about *that*, but I do plan to eat a lot of lasagna."

She laughs and we hang up, and after I've closed Fiona's phone, I stare at it and try to sort through what I'm feeling.

Mom's been so strong through all this.

So positive.

I, on the other hand, have been stormy and dark and defeated.

And now suddenly she's falling apart, and *I'm* telling *her* everything's okay.

It's like she's reached the end of her leg of the relay.

She gave it her all.

She's exhausted.

Collapsing.

I know what that feels like, and I know what this means.

It's my turn to hold the baton.

chapter 6

SOMEHOW I WIND UP STANDING in Angelo's crowded foyer for nearly twenty minutes while half a dozen two-legged people sit.

"Unbelievable," Fiona whispers as we finally follow the hostess to a table. "What is wrong with people?"

"It's okay," I tell her, but I'm relieved to be seated. Relieved to have left the foyer and the awkward glances of a mom who wouldn't actually look at me, and her kid who wouldn't stop.

We open our menus, but it's just a formality.

I'm getting the lasagna.

She's getting the eggplant parmesan.

"Oh!" she says, snapping her menu closed. "They've added mandarin chicken salad to the lunch menu."

"They have?" I ask, searching the menu.

She laughs. "Not here; at school!"

The waiter returns shortly to take our orders, and when he's gone, I sip my water and ask, "So what else is new at school?"

Fiona's eyes get wide.

I never ask about school.

I hate hearing about it; hate thinking about it. I break out in a cold sweat every time she starts chatting about it.

She reaches across the white tablecloth and nearly knocks over the single-carnation centerpiece as she grabs for my wrist. "You're coming back! Really? You're ready?" She bounces in her seat. "Finally, finally, finally!"

I look down. "I don't know if I'll ever be *ready*." I glance at her. "But I think I'm ready to try."

She bounces again, saying, "Tomorrow would be perfect! It's Friday. One day, then the weekend . . . You can get your feet wet, you know?" Her cheeks flush and she covers her mouth with a hand.

"Don't worry about it," I tell her, then shake my head. "But *tomorrow*?" The thought sends me into a panic.

"Look," she says softly, "you can put it off, but that'll just make it worse."

I think about this, about what Kaylee said, about how I've pushed away everyone I know because I'm always thinking, No. Finally I give a little nod and say, "It *would* only be one day, and then I'd have all weekend to get over people staring or ignoring or—"

"Or putting their foot in their mouth?"

I grin at her. "Yeah. That too."

"So is this a yes?"

I take a deep breath. "This is a maybe-yes."

Fiona laughs. "That's a big improvement over absolutely-no."

The waiter brings some steaming bread, which I'm happy to dive into. "So," I say, "catch me up."

Fiona grabs some bread. "Oh! Well! First off, everyone misses you. They ask me every day how you're doing."

"Really?" It comes out quiet. Like I'm hurt.

Which I guess I kind of am.

Fiona leans forward. "Of course they do!"

I shrug.

She frowns a little. "When you're gloomy and won't talk to people, they don't know what to do, okay? It's not their fault."

I look away. "I know."

"So, yes. Everyone misses you and asks about you and wants to know when you're coming back." She eyes me and says, "Gavin's asked about you at least three times."

"Gavin?" I shake my head. "Why? Does he need more information for his story?"

"He seems sincere, but . . ." Her voice trails off and she scowls.

"But what?"

She shakes her head.

"Just tell me."

She takes a deep breath, then blurts, "Merryl's managed to work her magic on him."

I feel myself flush. "They're going *out?*"

She rolls her eyes. Frowns. Rips apart her bread.

And then she nods.

After I compose myself, I say, "Look. Get real—he wasn't interested in me when I had *two* legs."

"What does that matter? You're the same person!"

No, I think as I sip my water, *I'm not.*

"Well, forget about him," she says. "What do *you* want to know about?"

This is a good question, and it's one I really don't have an answer to. I want to know everything about school.

And nothing about it.

It hurts to realize how unnecessary I am. From what little I've let Fiona tell me, school life seems the same as always. Track meets happen. The same flitty people are still flitting about. The same teachers are keeping to their same routines. The same lunchtime activities and rallies and club meetings still take place.

I fell off, but the merry-go-round keeps moving.

Lucy *died*, but the merry-go-round keeps moving.

Still. As much as thinking this upsets me, I'm starting to see that I need the merry-go-round much more than it needs me, and in the end my choice is to hop back on or get left in the dust.

So I take a deep breath and ask about the one thing that means the most to me.

The one thing I absolutely don't want to hear about.

"How's track?"

All her little fidgeting motions stop. She studies me a moment, then says, "We lost to Mount Vernon by six points. They swept the four hundred and won the four-by-four-hundred. It lost us the meet."

I have a twinge of comfort.

Maybe the merry-go-round at least slowed down with me gone.

"Did Marcy pick up my leg?" I ask.

Her mouth drops open and she blinks at me.

I blink too, realizing what I've just said. "I meant my leg of the relay!"

"I know what you meant," she says, and her face is twitching all over the place.

I snicker, then blurt out, "Did she pick up my leg!" and suddenly we're both hysterical.

I wipe my eyes with my napkin, and somewhere inside me I can feel a shift.

I'm turning a corner.

Leaving one long, hard section of track behind me.

I smile at Fiona.

It feels so, so good.

chapter 7

AFTER LUNCH FIONA HELPS ME organize the homework that she's continued to collect for me.

Six classes, three weeks . . . it's a daunting amount of work.

But Fiona's upbeat and optimistic, and since we have five out of six classes together, she's very familiar with the assignments.

"You know what?" she says after she's helped me make a checklist for each of the courses. "There's no reason you should have to do all those assignments. Some of them are total busywork."

"So what are you saying?"

"I'm saying that tomorrow we'll ask every teacher which assignments they'll let you slide on." She shakes her head. "Look how much you have to do. This is crazy!"

"So I shouldn't do any of them yet?"

She thinks a minute, then says, "Start with the math, but only do the odds. You know, half of them? You can check your answers in the back of the book, and if you're getting it, just move on."

I frown. "I don't know if Ms. Rucker's going to go for that."

"If she doesn't, she's ridiculous. Tell *her* to lose a leg and come back with all her homework done."

Mom comes into the family room. "Who are we discussing?"

Fiona and I exchange glances. "Ms. Rucker," Fiona grumbles. "She's such a machine."

"That's your math teacher, right?" Mom's trying to be casual, but she's beside herself that I'm organizing my schoolwork. She's had several conversations with my counselor about me making up work and returning to school, but I've been a complete brick wall about it. "Is there anything I can do to help?" she asks brightly.

I shake my head. "I think we've got things under control."

"How about some drinks, then? Apple juice, water, soda, Gatorade . . . ?"

"Apple juice," Fiona and I say together, and when Mom leaves, Fiona puts aside my newly organized binder and sets me up with paper, pencil, and my math book. "You want to get going on that while I park right here and do my homework?"

"Yes, ma'am," I say with a laugh, because it's obvious she's not going to take no for an answer.

We work diligently and I make good progress, especially with Fiona tutoring me through the math problems. And even though I'm having no trouble concentrating, I'm surprised to catch Fiona spacing out a couple of times.

The third time I notice it, I ask, "What are you thinking about?"

She says, "Huh?" then flutters off some answer that makes very little sense.

"What?"

Just then Mom comes into the room and asks Fiona to stay for dinner, but Fiona says, "I . . . I can't. I've got to get home. Tons to do!"

I want to ask, Like what? but in the back of my mind I'm getting the picture.

Fiona's planning cupcakes and streamers and banners.

Loudspeaker announcements and music.

She's planning my return to school.

In a flash, Fiona has packed up and is whirlwinding out of the room. "I will be here a little after seven tomorrow morning!" she says, pointing at me. "Be ready!" Then she darts from the room.

Mom chases after her and catches her out on the walkway, and now it's my turn to watch through the window.

Mom hugs her.

Holds her cheeks.

They talk and laugh and hug again, and then Fiona's hurrying to her car and Mom's waving goodbye.

"She is one amazing friend," my mother says as she comes back into the family room.

I nod.

"You're really lucky to have her."

I nod again.

And I would say more, but once again I'm overwhelmed.

This time in a good way.

chapter 8

I CAN'T SLEEP. I've got a mixture of butterflies and panic.

So I get up, get my history book, and start reading.

Eventually it puts me to sleep.

"Sweetheart!" my mother whispers, softly shaking my shoulder.

I turn a groggy eye toward the clock.

5:45.

I definitely need more sleep.

My mind stumbles to a comforting conclusion: I can always try going back to school . . . later.

Like Monday.

Or Tuesday.

Or next Friday.

Or—

"Jessica!" Mom's shaking my shoulder again.

I will her to go away, but I'm too tired to project much resistance. "I know," I murmur, but somewhere in the fog of my mind I'm aware that I don't know what I know. Whatever it is can't be much.

"Were you up all night reading?"

"A lot of it," I murmur.

She takes the history book off the bed. "Homework is not that important!" she scolds.

I grunt, then hide under the covers.

I just want to sleep.

Escape.

"Jessica," she says, gently pulling the covers off my head. "It's important that you go to school today."

"I'm too tired," I tell her, and pull a blanket over my head.

And then I remember.

Fiona.

Fiona and her cupcakes and banners and welcome-back balloons.

I groan and peek out of the covers. "Please tell me she's not making a big deal out of this."

Mom studies me, then lets a little smile escape. "You know her better than that."

"Ohhhhh," I groan, and sit up.

Mom kisses me on the head. "Would a shower help?"

I check the clock. It's almost six. "I don't have time."

"Then I'll start on breakfast," she says, and leaves me to get myself together.

I stretch out my leg and start on my morning physical therapy. It's become second nature to me. I used to do it because I had to, but now I do it because it helps me feel like I've still got a working body. Stretch, resistance, strengthen. I do both legs, both arms. I use towels, bands, and hand weights. It helps wake me up.

Next I do a quick sponge bath in the downstairs bath-room, fix my hair, then dress in a long-sleeved T, a hoodie vest, and my softest jeans. I pin the right leg up. It makes the situation more obvious, but really, there's no hiding what I'm missing and it bugs me to have the extra fabric flopping around.

"You look great!" Mom gushes as I hop to the kitchen table.

"Good morning, sweetheart," Dad says, and puts the newspaper aside.

Mom's big on traditional breakfast, so there's sausage, toast, and scrambled eggs, plus orange juice and milk. "Kaylee! Breakfast!" she calls at full volume. "Kaylee! You're going to be late!"

I start on my breakfast and hope that Kaylee appears for more than her usual bite-and-run. I want to try to start over with her. Maybe tell her the picked-up-my-leg story.

But Kaylee doesn't appear, and breakfast with Dad's a little awkward. I don't know why. We small-talk between pockets of silence, but it's strange. It's like he wants to say something, but he's holding back.

Then, just as Kaylee's footsteps are finally pounding down the stairs, Dad asks, "Do you think you'll see your coach today?"

"Uh . . . I don't know. I hope so."

"Good," he says, but there's an edge to his voice.

I rest my fork and study him. "It's not his fault, Dad. Kyro's a great guy. Fiona says I might have bled to death if it wasn't for him."

Dad gives a solemn nod. "I know."

"Then why are you mad at him?"

Mom shoots him a don't-even-go-there look as Kaylee blasts into the kitchen. "You're really going to school?" Kaylee asks.

"I'm trying it out," I tell her with a smile.

She stops. "Do that," she says, pointing at my face. "Do that right there and everything will be fine." She hugs me and whispers "I'm sorry about yesterday" in my ear.

Dad uses Kaylee's interruption to beat a speedy exit, and then the doorbell rings.

"Gotta run!" Kaylee says, gobbling down two bites of eggs and a swig of juice.

I ask Mom why Dad's mad at Kyro, but she says, "It's nothing for you to be concerned about."

"*What's* nothing to be concerned about?"

But it's not Kaylee's ride at the door—it's mine. "Fiona! Come in, come in," my mom calls, completely sweeping my question out of the kitchen.

"You ready?" Fiona asks, and she's beaming with excitement.

Suddenly the butterflies are back.

So is the fear.

But I nod, take a deep breath, and stand.

I'm really sore from all my activity yesterday, and my armpits are chafed from my trip to Angelo's. So after I brush my teeth and collect my things, I don't put up much of a fuss about using the wheelchair.

"Just be queen for the day," Fiona says, thinking she needs to convince me.

"It's a big campus," my mom chimes in.

"Fine," I tell them.

So Fiona and my mom scurry to get me, my backpack, and the wheelchair into Fiona's car. Mom gives me a kiss and tells me, "I'm so proud of you."

I smile at her and close the car door, and as we pull away from the curb, I roll down the window and wave like I'm a queen on parade.

She laughs.

I laugh.

So far, so good.

chapter 9

I'M NOT LAUGHING when we pull into the student parking lot. Instead, my heart's hammering inside my chest, and I'm desperate to go home.

I know I'm being irrational.

Still, I'm having a complete panic attack.

There are already swarms of people at school. Fiona and I had planned to arrive before seven-thirty, but it's already seven-forty.

Everything takes longer with only one leg.

Everything.

"It'll be okay," Fiona says as she pulls up the parking brake. "Give me a minute. I'll be around with your throne."

I'm breaking out in a cold sweat. "We've only got ten minutes to get to class. Maybe we should—"

"We'll be *fine*," she calls as she zips around to the hatchback. She pulls out the collapsed wheelchair and says over the backseat, "Jessica, really, this is the best thing you could be doing. You'll see. It'll be fine."

I manage to hobble out of the car as she opens up the chair and wheels it over to the passenger door.

"There you go!" she says, and I sit.

I'm not used to the wheelchair. It seems too small and too big, too precarious and too safe, all at the same time.

My left leg feels cramped by the footrest.

My right leg feels lost at sea.

The jeans leg is pinned up, and I suddenly want it down.

Maybe I won't look like such a pathetic freak.

I undo the safety pins while Fiona gets our backpacks. "Ready, Your Majesty?" she asks, and when I nod, she straps on her backpack and rests mine in my lap. "Then let's roll!"

The pant leg flaps as she hurries me toward the school entrance.

Flap, flap, flap.

It bothers me.

Flusters me.

Then totally freaks me out.

"Stop!" I cry.

She keeps pushing as she asks, "What's wrong?"

"STOP!"

She does stop, and comes around to face me. "We're almost there," she says softly. "It'll be all right. I *promise* you it'll be all right."

I manage to choke out, "My pant leg is driving me crazy."

She watches me pin it back up, then asks, "You okay now?"

I nod, but I'm not okay. I'm anything but okay.

I know it's not my fault. I know I haven't done anything wrong. I know it's irrational. But still, I'm mortified.

Mortified to be me.

chapter 10

My DOWNWARD SPIRAL IS INTERRUPTED by Shandall Norwood. "Jessica?" she asks, coming toward us from the left. "Jessica!" she squeals, and charges at me, her arms spread wide. "Girl, you're back!" she cries, smothering me in a hug.

Shandall is a sophomore, is fast enough to run the 100 for varsity, and is potentially deadly with a discus. When she hits her release right, the discus soars, but once in a while she gets turned around and sends it off in the wrong direction. All of us have learned to stand clear when Shandall's spinning toward her release.

I return her hug and feel a bit calmer. "Good to see you too," I mumble into her shoulder.

She pulls back and smiles, and then . . . what is there to say?

It's not like I'll be going to track practice.

It's not like we have anything else in common.

"We've got to get moving," Fiona says after an awkward few seconds. "Can't have her tardy on her first day back!"

So Shandall waves and hurries off, and Fiona rolls me

across the parking lot and around the corner to the school's entrance arch and onto campus. Fiona's moving fast and chattering away. "We're lucky we don't go to one of those schools where everything's, like, enclosed, and the halls are really crowded, and you have to go up and down levels to get to class."

She's right, but what I'm thinking is, *How will I do this in the rain?*

We enter the courtyard, and as Fiona pushes me along the sidewalk, I see the first signs that she's been a busy bee. On our right is the outdoor theater—a Greek-style semicircle of stepped cement seats going down to a stage—an area that the upper classes tend to dominate during lunchtime. Along the far wall are balloons and a large WELCOME BACK JESSICA!!! banner.

I smile over my shoulder at Fiona, and she leans forward and whispers, "Gavin helped me put it up."

The warning bell rings as she hurries me along to first period. A couple of people wave and call hello, but mostly it's people shortcutting across the lawns, hurrying to beat the next bell.

"You are the best friend ever," I tell her. "I love the banner." I twist around farther. "What time did you *get* here?"

She laughs like, Oh, you have no idea, and simply says, "Early."

Liberty High is laid out like a wagon wheel, with the courtyard as the hub. In the old days the school was much smaller, but as time's gone by, more and more portable classrooms have been added to the fields behind the school. Each segment of the wheel is called a wing, and every wing is for a certain subject area and is named with a number. Math is in the 900 Wing, science is in the 800 Wing, English is in the 200 Wing. . . .

Not the most creative, but easy to figure out.

Fiona rolls me into a portable unit in the 200 Wing. It's really just the educational version of a double-wide trailer, and like all the portable units, it's got a ramp. A long, zigzag ramp that's always annoyed me. It's a time killer when you're running late, a bottleneck when the release bell rings; and it's noisy. *Clomp, clomp, clomp*, people come up it in the middle of class to deliver messages and whatnot. It always wrecks my concentration when we're testing.

Plus it's ugly. Painted wood, pipe guardrail . . . Some teachers try, but there's nothing anyone can do to camouflage it. It is what it is.

And what it is now is my only way into the classroom.

This bothers me more than it should. When I was a freshman, my friends and I used to swing under the guardrail to get inside the classroom, leap over it to get out. It was just quicker.

Teachers scolded it out of us, or maybe we just grew up. But as Fiona rolls me up the ramp, I see my options as closed.

I can no longer catapult.

Or swing.

Or slide.

I can only roll.

Something about this makes me grab the wheels and push.

"Careful," Fiona says. "Don't get your fingers caught!"

"Just let me do it," I tell her, but when she lets go, I

discover that pushing myself is not easy. The motion's all forearms and triceps, and I don't seem to have much strength in them.

I also can't steer very well, and by the time I've maneuvered the chair to face the second half of the ramp, I'm holding up traffic. "Go ahead," I grumble to the people waiting, and I let Fiona finish pushing me inside. And then I'm distracted by something I hadn't even considered.

Where do I sit?

Am I supposed to get out of the wheelchair and hop over to my regular seat?

Should I stay in the wheelchair at the back of the classroom?

How am I supposed to take notes?

Ms. Aloi comes to my rescue. "Oh, Jessica!" she says, moving toward the back of the classroom. "It's so good to see you! No one seemed to know when you'd be returning. . . ." She drags an empty desk alongside my wheelchair and says, "I'll get them to deliver a table for you, but for today, will this work?"

"Sure," I tell her, and try to smile like everything's just dandy.

"Uh, Ms. Aloi?" Fiona says, signaling me to get out my English assignments sheet. "Here's a list of the homework Jessica's missed. She hasn't been able to do it—I'm sure you can understand that. And now she's overwhelmed by everything she has to catch up on, so we're wondering which of these you'll excuse her from."

Ms. Aloi looks directly at Fiona.

Fiona holds her gaze. "She has six classes, Ms. Aloi." She shakes the list a little and says, "They're all like this." Then she gives Ms. Aloi a pleading look. "There must be *some* leeway?"

Ms. Aloi takes the list and smiles at me. "We'll work something out." The tardy bell has rung, so she heads to the front of the class calling, "Good morning, everybody! Let's welcome Jessica back!"

Everyone claps and whistles, and a couple of people even stand up.

Fiona grins and gives me a wink as she moves to her assigned seat. It's a wink that means something specific:

You can make it.

You can do this.

One down, five to go.

chapter 11

EVERYWHERE I GO, I feel like the elephant in the room. A lot of people do say hi and welcome me back, but a lot more don't.

Fiona notices it, too, whispering, "Maturity check!" in my ear when people pretend that I'm not there.

I feel myself shutting down.

Withdrawing.

She gives me the same advice Kaylee did. "Smile," she whispers. "Be open. If you're friendly, they'll be friendly."

This is not easy for me. And it seems backward. But I don't want to be treated like I'm invisible, so I try.

I also try to speak for myself and ask my teachers to excuse me from some of the homework. They're all very nice about it, but what's left is still overwhelming. Especially since I'm also diving into the middle of new lessons and new homework assignments.

After science class is over, Mr. Vedder returns my assignment list, and I'm surprised to see that instead of having me do a big project, he's allowing me to submit a five-hundred-word essay, and he's whittled my worksheets down to three.

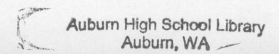

"I wish I could excuse you from all of it," he says as I'm checking it over. "What's left is the bare minimum for the curriculum."

I'm so relieved to be excused from the project that I gush, "No, this is great! You have no idea how much this helps, Mr. Vedder!"

He gives me a kind smile. "I'm just glad you're back, Jessica. Anything you need, you just ask, okay?"

I nod and thank him and tell him to have a nice weekend, but as Fiona starts pushing me toward the door, he asks, "How are your parents doing with all this?"

The question's quiet. Like he's not really sure he should be asking but can't seem to help himself.

It's also the first truly personal question I've been asked all day, and an odd one because Mr. Vedder doesn't even know my parents.

My skin prickles.

Why is he asking me this?

What business is it of his?

But then my mind flashes to the pictures of his daughter, Hannah, on his desk; to his stories about Hannah catching lizards in their driveway; pranking him on April Fools'; crashing her bike and breaking her arm.

Suddenly I get it.

He doesn't know my parents, but he *is* a parent.

So I tell him the truth.

"It's hard," I say softly. "Ups and downs, just like me."

He nods, then takes a deep breath and lets it out as he says, "I can't even imagine."

On our way down Mr. Vedder's ramp, Fiona whispers, "That was awkward."

"It was fine," I tell her.

It's lunchtime, and I'm famished. But Fiona's not heading toward the courtyard; she's steering me *away* from it.

"Hey, where are we going?" I ask over my shoulder.

"To lunch," she says with a mischievous grin.

"Lunch" is located in Coach Kyro's portable classroom.

"Lunch" consists of pizza, salads, cupcakes, sodas, cookies, and licorice.

"Lunch" is decorated with balloons and streamers and WELCOME BACK JESSICA written all over the whiteboards.

"Lunch" is a gathering of runners and friends and coaches. "SURPRISE!" they all shout, and blow party horns or shower me with confetti.

"Lunch" makes me cry.

I suddenly realize how much I miss these people.

It's not just running.

It's the team.

"You guys are the best," I finally choke out, wiping the tears away.

Someone starts up with "For she's a jolly good fellow . . . ," which makes absolutely no sense, but it doesn't matter. And then someone shouts, "Speech! Speech!" like I've done something great instead of survived something awful.

I shake my head and wave off that crazy idea and simply say, "Eat! Eat!"

Everyone laughs and dives for food, because, come on— when is a runner *not* hungry?

As Fiona delivers me a plate with salad and a slice of pepperoni-pineapple, Kyro pulls up a desk beside me and says, "You have no idea how much we've missed you."

I nod and attempt a smile. He looks grayer than I remember. Older. I notice a woven green-and-black name bracelet tied around his wrist.

The letters spell "Lucy."

I look away, feeling bad that I haven't spoken to him since the accident. I feel bad that he tried and I didn't; that he came to the hospital and I didn't want to see him. After three years of him believing in me, pushing me, tailoring my workouts, I'd become the fastest 400-meter sprinter in the league.

And I never even bothered to call him back.

"I'd really like to talk to you sometime," he says.

I nod. "Me too. I'm sorry that I've been so . . . shut down."

He shakes his head. "Who can blame you, Jess? Come on."

I look at him and blurt out, "What's going on with you and my dad?"

He seems to weigh things in his mind, then says, "There's a tangle of insurance issues, and things are not resolving as quickly as either of us would like. I'm afraid your dad thinks I could be doing more to pressure things along, but it really is out of my hands."

"It's about *insurance?*"

He nods. "It'll get straightened out, but these things can take time."

I'm baffled.

My dad's been down on Kyro about *insurance*?

How could that possibly be the coach's responsibility?

But then I start wondering: So who paid for the hospital?

Or the ambulance?

Or the physical therapist?

Or the wheelchair or the crutches or the shrinker socks or the . . . or the *anything*?

Before this, it never even crossed my mind. I thought it was just . . . taken care of.

"Hey," he says, standing. "I sure didn't mean to put a damper on your party. Enjoy yourself, would you? We've waited a long time to celebrate your return." He turns to my teammates, huddled around the food. "Hey! People! Get over here and talk to Jessica, or I'll make you do laps!"

When Kyro barks, runners listen. In an instant I'm surrounded by love and chatter and half-eaten pizza. And despite the weirdness of my first day back, I'm happy to be there.

Happy to see that I've been missed.

chapter 12

MY ONLY CLASS WITHOUT FIONA is math, and it's the last period of the day. I have algebra II/trig; Fiona's down the wing in pre-calculus. She swears she's not taking calculus next year, and I refuse to take pre-calc. Enough is enough.

After fifth, Fiona rushes me clear across campus to the 900 Wing and is panting as she rolls me up to the front of the classroom, where Ms. Rucker is erasing the board.

Ms. Rucker is the one teacher we're both nervous about. She *is* a machine. Never smiling, never flexing, never sharing anything personal.

Her life is all about numbers, and her demeanor is as severe as her haircut, which is a dark, straight, asymmetrical bob. I'm sure there's a real person inside her somewhere, but after having her for algebra I and II, I've quit trying to find her. I'm just looking forward to being done with math, and being done with her.

She knows who Fiona is. Not only did she have her in class last year, but Fiona's been getting my assignments from her. And obviously she knows who I am. Still, when she turns from erasing the board, she doesn't say anything like, Welcome back, or It's good to see you. She simply sizes me up.

So I'm a little flustered as I go into my spiel about cutting back my homework, and during it Ms. Rucker's expression never cracks. She just watches me closely.

Absorbs.

It's like data in, process, response.

Only the response seems to be taking a very long time.

Obviously, she doesn't like the data I'm feeding her and has no intention of returning anything but *Request denied.* So I open my binder and produce the assignments I've completed and say, "I've been doing the odds and checking my answers. It's going to be a lot of work to catch up *and* keep up with the new assignments."

She takes my papers, looks them over, then says, "Doing the odds seems reasonable."

And that's it.

No smile.

No nod.

No quiver of any emotion whatsoever.

She simply returns to wiping the boards clean and asks, "Will you be sitting with Rosa?"

For a moment my mind's a blank. Then I realize she means the special-needs girl who sits at the back of the classroom.

The girl in the motorized wheelchair.

The girl who rarely talks and, when she does, is very hard to understand.

I didn't even know her name was Rosa.

"There's plenty of room at that table," Ms. Rucker says without looking over her shoulder.

Inside, I panic.

Yes, I'm missing a leg, but the rest of me is . . . well, it's *normal*.

Do people think I'm special-needs now?

Is that how they see me?

No! They can't!

But . . . but if I start sitting with special-needs kids, that *is* what people will think.

It just is.

Ms. Rucker turns and gives me a cool, blank look.

She wants an answer.

My mind is a flurry of contradictions. I want to lie and say I'm nearsighted. That I need to be up front in my own chair. That I hop just fine.

But I also think about my terror in returning to school. Feeling like a freak.

Is that how Rosa feels?

I've never stared at her, but I have . . . overlooked her.

No—the truth is, I've totally acted like she isn't there.

It's been easier.

Less uncomfortable.

For me.

"Sure," I tell Ms. Rucker. "I'd be happy to sit with Rosa."

She cocks her head ever so slightly, then turns to finish wiping the board.

So I get situated alongside Rosa, and Fiona dashes off to class. Then the tardy bell rings and everyone falls silent, waiting for Ms. Rucker to speak.

There's no let's-welcome-Jessica-back. Just business as usual: homework out, papers exchanged, lesson reviewed.

Midway through this process Rosa surprises me by committing a cardinal sin—she passes me a note.

I read it and sin right back. And after several exchanges Rosa's told me that she has been in a wheelchair her whole life, that she *can* walk but only with arm crutches, and that she was born with cerebral palsy. I also find out that she's only a freshman, loves sushi, thinks math is easy, and eats lunch in Room 402.

You can join us, she writes. *We're fun!*

I also learn that she already knew my name. And Fiona's.

Fiona seems very nice, she tells me, adding a big, long-lashed smiley.

She's amazing, I write back, adding long, curly hair to the smiley.

Rosa gives me a lopsided grin, then writes, *When do you get your leg?*

Depends, I scribble back. *Maybe next week?*

Already? WOW! Congratulations! You are SO LUCKY!

My eyes sting when I read that, and it makes something in me break.

Or connect.

Or just *change*, somehow.

I suddenly really get that I *am* lucky. I'll never do a fifty-five flat in the 400 again, but I will stand on my own again.

This wheelchair won't be with me every day of my life.

chapter 13

AFTER SCHOOL FIONA'S ROLLING ME across campus in the direction of the courtyard when she says, "I just realized something."

"What's that?"

"Guess who wasn't at your party today?"

"Uh . . . who?"

"Merryl."

I shift my backpack in my lap. "Did I miss her? No!" I twist to glance at Fiona. "Forget about her, would you?"

Fiona grunts. "Hard to do."

"Look, I know you hate her, but I'm starting to think you're obsessing about her because you like *him*."

She stops wheeling and comes around to look me right in the eyes. "What kind of friend do you think I am? *You're* the one who likes him. The whole thing bugs me because he should be with someone like you, not her!"

"Fiona, please. Stop this."

But she doesn't. "I—*we*—thought he was smart. You know, *principled*. Remember his speech when he was running for class president? You said it was the most amazing thing you'd ever heard. And it was!" She starts pushing me again. "How could he let himself be snowed by Merryl?"

"Uh . . . she's gorgeous?"

She grunts again. "Guys are so shallow."

"Look. It goes both ways. Most girls don't like Gavin because of some speech, or because of his op-ed pieces in the school paper, or because he started a townwide warmth drive. They like him because he's cute."

"Well, see? You're different. And I'm sorry. I know I've been kind of annoying about him. It just makes me mad to see *her* with him when she's such a princess and you've gone through so much."

I twist around again. "Well, keep your cool, because here they come."

Gavin and Merryl are quite a distance across the courtyard, but they're on the same walkway we're on, and they're definitely closing in. Merryl is linked to Gavin in her classic way: both of her arms hugging one of his as she looks up adoringly at him.

It's strange, but it doesn't really bother me.

I guess I've got bigger issues now than clinging to an old crush.

Still, what I really want to do is steer clear of them. Go in a different direction. Go four-wheelin' across the grass. I just don't want to have to deal with him *or* her.

But as I'm suggesting this to Fiona, Gavin notices us. He stops for an instant, then hurries toward us, leaving Merryl clinging to air.

"Jessica!" he calls.

"I *hate* being a charity case," I grumble.

He smiles as he approaches. "I've been watching for you all day! I thought you'd be in the courtyard at lunch."

Fiona's right about his chin scruff. It gives him an edge.

A very attractive edge.

As if he needed it.

Merryl's already scurried over, and the first thing she does is latch on to Gavin again. "Hi, Jessie!" she says. "S*oooo* good to see you!"

I can feel myself bristle.

Like I need her phony friendliness?

Fiona moves up beside me and keeps her focus on Gavin. "The track team had a party for her in Kyro's room. The whole team was there." She eyes Merryl. "Well, *almost* the whole team."

Gavin looks at Merryl, who releases him with one hand so she can hold back a gasp of regret. "Oh, I'm so sorry! I completely forgot!!"

"Easy to do, I suppose," Fiona says, turning a sarcastic eye toward the big, bold WELCOME BACK banner in the Greek theater. She sweeps around behind me and says, "Well, we've got to get moving. Places to go, things to do."

"Wow," I gasp when we're out of earshot. "You were kinda brutal."

"I have never known anyone so phony and self-absorbed," she mutters. "Guys can be so dumb."

We get to the car and I'm suddenly tired.

"You made it," she says when we're both belted in. "How are you feeling?"

I laugh. "I'm feeling sorry for you that you have to go to track practice! You were up all night putting together this amazing day for me, and now you have to go do what? Wind sprints?"

She cranks the motor. "It's actually just a team meeting. And Kyro knows I'm going to be late."

"Just a team meeting?" But then I realize why. "Are the Glenwood Relays tomorrow?"

She nods.

As we drive along, I think about Gavin being with Merryl, and I'm surprised that it really *doesn't* bother me. Maybe it's the contrast between subjects. Gavin versus the Glenwood Relays—right after the last invitational meet, someone died.

Someone else lost her leg.

Besides, if Merryl's the kind of girl Gavin likes, then maybe I gave him too much credit.

These thoughts swirl inside me for a little while, and I let them stew. But in the end the conclusion doesn't change. I'm not just consoling myself, or fooling myself into believing I don't want him because my chances of having him have gone from slim to none.

It's really just simple.

I'm over Gavin Vance.

chapter 14

MOM'S WATCHING FOR ME when I get home.

I knew she would be.

She has SunChips and cheese waiting for me in the kitchen—my favorite after-school snack.

We sit and talk, and it makes me feel good that she's so interested in knowing all about my day, but honestly, how can I explain it? I tell her the basics—that my homework load is greatly reduced, that Fiona was amazing, that there was a big party for me in Kyro's room, and that people were nice to me—but I don't mention the stares or averted eyes. I don't tell her about Gavin, or Merryl, or Mr. Vedder's question, or Ms. Rucker's cool demeanor, or sitting with Rosa. I'm too tired to revisit any of the tough stuff.

But tired or not, there is one thing I have to know about.

"Mom . . . ?" I ask as she's refilling my juice glass.

"Yes, sweetheart?"

"Kyro mentioned there's a problem with insurance. What's going on? And why does Dad think it's Kyro's fault?"

The juice slows to a dribble as she looks directly at me. It runs down the pitcher, then drips onto the table. "He said that?"

"Yes."

The pitcher wobbles a bit as she puts it down. "He shouldn't have mentioned a thing." She shakes her head a little. "Your father will be furious."

"Why? I don't get that. I don't get it at all."

"Because you, of all people, shouldn't be worried or even *thinking* about insurance. He had no business telling you that there's a problem."

"He only told me because I asked."

"About insurance?"

"No. About why Dad's mad at him."

"Your father's not mad at *him*, really. He's mad at the situation, and I think that in the beginning Kyro got the brunt of that."

"Well, Dad made me think he was mad at Kyro, so I asked, okay?"

Mom sighs. "Well, now he will be."

"He'll be mad at Kyro? Look, none of this, *none* of it, is his fault. He's aged ten years since the wreck. He wears a Lucy bracelet, okay?"

Mom heaves another sigh.

"So tell me what's going on with insurance! I don't understand what the big problem is."

I stare at her as she considers this for what seems like an eternity. Finally she takes a deep breath and says, "It's nothing that time won't take care of. Everything will be okay. It's just that payment is clogged because the different insurance companies are dragging their feet, each pointing the finger at the other."

I frown at her. "What does that mean?"

She closes her eyes, takes another deep breath, holds it for another eternity, and finally says, "Jack Lowe didn't have insurance."

"The guy in the truck that hit us?"

"Right. See, normally, since the accident was his fault, his insurance company would pay your medical bills. But he didn't have insurance. His truck wasn't even legally registered. He had current tags, but the police think he peeled them off another vehicle to avoid getting stopped."

I let this sink in. "But . . . who does he work for? Don't *they* have insurance?"

She sighs. "He worked for himself. He was a freelance junk hauler and got paid by the job."

"So that's it? There's no insurance, no money?"

"Well, he's still liable, or his estate is now. And he did own property—a sizeable chunk of it up near Penn Lake, where his widow lives."

"So . . . what, then? Will she have to sell it to pay for the hospital bills?"

My mother nods. "Yes, but of course she doesn't want to, so she's hired a lawyer to fight it. Meanwhile, the school district and the bus company are both claiming no fault and so far haven't picked up any of the expenses."

"Wait. The busses aren't owned by the school?"

"That's right. Apparently they're owned by a subcontractor with separate insurance. It's all very complicated, with lots of people in lots of offices claiming it's not their liability."

A question hovers in my mind.

"But . . . don't *we* have insurance?"

My voice is small because I'm pretty sure I already know the answer.

"We do on your dad—health, life, disability. . . . We've got the works on him." She shakes her head and wipes the juice up with a napkin. "We *used* to have it for the rest of us, but the cost was so high that we let it go . . . and we never imagined this."

I let this all sink in, then ask, "So who's been paying the bills?"

Her lips pinch together as she breathes in through her nose. "As I said, it's going to take some time to sort this out."

"But meanwhile? And how much money are we talking about?"

"Meanwhile, it is *not* your job to worry about this. It will all work itself out, okay? Your sole focus should be getting back into life." She smiles at me. "Which it sounds like you did a great job of today."

I'm quiet. Thinking.

She gets that way too.

Then she stands and clears our paper plates. "If you don't mind," she says softly, "let's keep this conversation between the two of us. I don't know who your dad would be madder at—your coach or me."

Keeping it between us is not hard to do. Dad works late

and then is gone early. He hasn't been around much since I came home from the hospital, and now I understand why.

I still have to see doctors.

I still need to get a leg.

Someone has to pay the bills.

chapter 15

SATURDAY I SUBMERGE MYSELF in homework. I actually like it, which feels odd. Homework has always been something to dread.

Now it's something I can *do*.

I try hard not to think about the team running at the Glenwood Relays.

I try to block out memories of the fun we had there last year.

I try to block out how the last invitational ended.

Dad and Mom and Kaylee move me back into my bedroom on Sunday because I insist on it. I'm good at scooting up the stairs now. I hop around everywhere, or use the crutches. I can actually pinch a crutch with my armpit and carry something while I move.

And I discover crawling.

Rediscover, I suppose. I don't know what took me so long to try it. It's quicker than hopping, but I only do it on rugs or carpets—and only when I'm alone, because seeing me crawl really bothers my mom.

Sunday night I take a shower. It's gotten easier, especially now that Dad's bought a real shower seat and installed a step on either side of the tub curb so I don't have to land on the door guide.

I do my usual routine, then shut off the water and treat my stump the way I'm supposed to. I massage it, rough it up with the hand towel, beat it with the towel folded. . . . It can take a lot more pressure than it used to, and I push the towel therapy until I can really feel it.

Even with the rough treatment, there is no shooting pain. And the scar's red, but it's no longer tender or swollen. I still get phantom pains, but not as often, and they're not as severe. It's like my stump is giving up being angry. Giving up fighting back. Like it's ready for a truce.

I maneuver out of the shower, and as I'm dressing, I think about my leg.

Not the one I've lost.

The one they'll build me.

How does that work?

What will it be like?

Hank tried to explain it when I was in the hospital, but I couldn't bear to listen. He had a brochure with pictures of legs. They had plastic feet, a pipe for a calf. . . . They were Frankensteinish.

In my mind he became Hankenstein.

Somebody I didn't want to see.

But now . . . now the idea of a leg—any leg—seems better than crutching.

Or wheeling, or hopping, or scooting, or crawling.

What a liberating luxury walking would be.

It's the first time I've thought about this without someone else bringing it up. It's the first time I *haven't* thought that the only leg I want is the one I can't have.

It's the first time I've felt ready.

And suddenly I want it *now*.

PART III

Straightaway

chapter 1

MONDAY DURING SCIENCE a note from the office gets delivered to me. There's a single line scrawled beneath the checked REPORT TO OFFICE IMMEDIATELY box:

Dr. appt.

I'm a little stunned. I knew Mom was going to get me an appointment with Dr. Wells, but I wasn't expecting one so soon. I strap on my backpack, and Fiona helps me down the ramp. I'm crutching my way around school today, and it's been going okay, except for the ramps. I have a tough time with them, which I find strangely ironic.

"I'll be fine," I say to Fiona as she starts to follow me to the office. "You need to go in there and take notes for us, okay?" She hesitates, but I shoo her off and hobble across the campus.

It's quite a distance to the office, and I'm relieved to finally get there. The backpack has become heavier with every step, and my arms are sore. But my mom's waiting for me, full of energy. "Dr. Wells had an eleven-thirty cancellation. If we hurry, we'll make it!"

We do hurry. And we do make it. And then we fidget in the waiting room for almost an hour.

The meeting itself is short. When we're finally in an examining room, Dr. Wells appears almost immediately. "Hello, Jessica!" he says, then wheels over to me on his doctor's stool. He inspects my stump, prods it, measures it, then says, "Outstanding!" He whips a prescription pad from his white coat pocket. "You are definitely ready for a preparatory prosthesis, and in record time." He scribbles on the pad, then peels off the prescription and hands it to me. "Good work, and congratulations!"

He's already on his way out the door when my mom says, "So we take this to Hank Kruber?"

"Or any other prosthetist."

"Uh—who would you recommend?"

Dr. Wells stops in the open doorway. "Hank's a good choice. And you do want to stay local. Jessica will be needing regular adjustments—especially since she's almost certainly still growing."

When we get home, my mom looks up prosthetists in the phone book, and what she discovers is that if we are going to stay local, Hank Kruber is our only choice.

"Hankenstein's fine, Mom," I tell her.

She turns to look at me. "Hankenstein?"

I shrug. "My head was in a bad place in the hospital. He thought a pipe leg was something I should be thrilled about. But if he can get me walking, let's go."

"Hankenstein," she chuckles, then finds the number and makes the call.

When she's done, she says, "The receptionist was so nice! She'll work us in at ten tomorrow morning. She says to wear shorts."

So the next day I miss more school and report to Hankenstein's lab. It's on a busy part of Grand Avenue, behind a fenced-off gas station and next to a Laundromat. The asphalt parking lot is full of potholes and there's trash blown up against the building. A faded blue sign reads QUALITY ORTHOTICS AND PROSTHETICS, so we know we're in the right place; it just feels wrong.

My mom unstraps her seat belt. "Let's just go in and see what we think, okay?"

I nod and work myself and my crutches out of the passenger seat. I feel strange in shorts.

Vulnerable.

"If you don't like it here," she whispers as we near the entrance, "we'll take you someplace else."

I know she's just being nice and that I don't really have a choice. Still, I'm glad she said it.

The waiting room is set up like a doctor's office, only the chairs are plain molded plastic, and instead of carpeting there's chipped linoleum. There's an odd smell to the place, too. Not bad, just sort of . . . industrial.

An elderly couple is already in the waiting room. The man is in a wheelchair, and he's holding a fake leg across his lap. His wife is sitting beside him with her purse in her lap. They look us over without smiling or saying hello, and the old man seems very unhappy. Like he'd sooner hurl his leg than wear it.

We go up to the reception counter and I try to ban thoughts of my future from my mind.

I do not want to be a crabby old lady holding a leg in my lap.

I just don't.

The receptionist is younger than my mom. Actually, she's not that much older than I am. Maybe in her early twenties?

"Hi!" she says across the counter. "You must be Jessica!"

She's like sunshine through my cloud of uncertainty. I smile and nod, and since she's wearing a name tag, I say, "And you must be Chloe." We both laugh, and suddenly I feel more at ease. Nothing's changed but the vibe in the room, but it helps.

She gives my mom a clipboard with paperwork to fill out, then leans forward a little and says to me, "Hank will have you walking again in no time. He's really good."

I nod and smile, and in that moment I believe her.

Then my mom and I sit in the hard plastic chairs, and I'm confronted with the reality of the old man and his leg again.

He just sits there, sullen.

His wife just sits there, quiet.

Mom's completed about half the paperwork when Chloe appears in the waiting room. She's not wearing a nurse-type smock or shoes, just regular clothes—jeans, a knit top, and flats. The only thing that gives away that she works there is her name tag.

She smiles at the old man and says, "You can come on back, Mr. Benson."

His response is a frown and a grunt. It is also, apparently, a signal for his wife to roll him out of the waiting room.

Chloe tosses me a little shrug and follows them.

Then we sit there for what seems like an eternity. Chloe splits her time between the desk and . . . somewhere in the back. She apologizes several times for how long it's taking and finally comes out into the waiting room and sits beside me. "He's almost done." She looks at my mom. "I really didn't think it would take this long. I'm sorry."

"That's all right," my mom says. "I appreciate you working us in."

Chloe looks at me, looks away, looks at me again, and finally says, "Things will change. From here on, they'll get better."

She seems to be choosing her words carefully. Like each one carries a meaning beyond its definition.

She gives a nervous laugh. "I don't usually come out and accost the patients, sorry! It's just that Hank told me about you and . . . and I can relate."

Again, there's more to these words than I can puzzle out. I'm trying, but I'm not quite there.

My mom's trying too. "Was somebody in your family in an accident?"

Chloe shakes her head. She knocks on her leg with a solid *clunk, clunk*. "I'm a BK amputee too. I lost mine to cancer when I was a kid."

From the hallway we hear, "Chloe?"

She jumps up and hurries across the room, and in the blink of an eye she's gone, leaving me with my jaw dangling.

chapter 2

MR. BENSON LEAVES IN HIS WHEELCHAIR, his leg still in his lap. He looks even grumpier than he did before.

"Remember to practice with it, Mr. Benson," Chloe calls after him.

He doesn't say a word.

Chloe smiles at me. "Your turn."

As she leads us down the hallway, I watch her legs. Her movements are smooth. Assured.

Part of me doesn't quite believe she's got a fake leg.

The rest of me is enormously encouraged.

She takes us to a small room with a patient table and a service sink. The floor is stained dusty white. Like a chalkboard that won't come clean. It's not just the floor, either. The cupboard doors, the sink, the chairs . . . there's chalky whiteness everywhere.

"Just sit up here," Chloe says, pulling fresh paper over the table. "Hank will take some measurements, do a cast"—she smiles at me—"nothing that hurts."

When she's gone, my mom whispers, "That's amazing! I sure can't tell—"

Hank walks in. He's the same guy I remember from my hospital nightmare: stocky, bald, partially preoccupied. Like half of him is somewhere else.

I notice his shoes, his pants, his shirt . . . they're all smudged chalky white.

"Jessica!" he says, like the other half of him has finally arrived. He seems genuinely happy to see me. "Good to see you looking so well!" He turns to my mom. "Hello, Mrs. Carlisle. How are you?"

Mom nods. But he's waiting for a real answer, so she says, "Better than the last time you saw me."

"Good." He scoots a chair up to me and says, "So let's get you fitted for a leg, shall we?"

He has me take off my shrinker sock, and my left shoe and sock, too. Then he starts measuring. He uses tools like I've seen my dad use. A metal caliper. A tape measure. Something that looks just like a carpenter's square. He takes all sorts of measurements of my stump side, and of my good side, too. And when he's all done, he nods and says, "And what kind of shoe do you normally wear?"

I point to my running shoe. "These."

He picks up the shoe and makes a note of the size, then says, "Okay. We're ready to make a cast of your residual limb. From that we'll be able to make a plaster model, and from *that* we'll build your first socket."

Mom asks, "The socket's the part that goes over her . . . over the residual limb?"

"That's right. Once we've got a comfortable socket, we'll add the pylon and the foot. But first things first. We do a cast." He goes to a cupboard, pulls out a box of supplies, and hands me a long, simple belt with a sliding clasp. "Fasten this around your waist," he says, then proceeds to untangle three adjustable straps that have little clamps on both ends. He puts the straps aside, then produces a short, very thin stocking, which he pulls onto my stump. It's smooth and soft. Almost silky.

"We cover your residual leg with this first," he says, "because it makes it much easier to remove the cast." Next he attaches the stocking to the belt around my waist with the three straps, and when he's sure it's secure and the stocking is on smooth and tight, he says, "Just a few markings and we're ready!"

Right on top of the stocking, he begins marking places. Around my knee. Along what's left of my shin. My scar. Points where bones stick out . . .

The pencil he's using is blue, and when he's done, the stocking looks like a little kid scribbled on it.

"These markings will transfer to the cast," he explains. "They'll show me where we can put pressure, and also where we should relieve it."

Next he fills a small bowl with water and brings it and two rolls of chalky-looking white gauze over to the table. "Have you ever had a cast?"

I shake my head.

"It doesn't take long." He dunks one of the gauzy rolls into the bowl of water, and when it's wet, he starts wrapping it around my leg, spiraling from the knee down to the end of the stump and back up. "This has plaster of Paris in it," he tells me as he wraps. "The water creates an exothermic reaction—do you feel it warming up?"

I nod because my stump is getting warmer and warmer. It's not uncomfortable. More like a hot towel wrap.

He uses both rolls, then tells me to relax my leg and begins massaging the plaster of Paris around. "We need good contact," he says, "so we get an accurate impression." When he's done massaging the plaster, he smooths it down with his hands, then presses his thumbs around the bottom part of my kneecap, getting a good impression of that area. "There," he says. "Now we wait a few minutes for it to harden, and that's it. Easy, huh?"

He cleans up while we wait. There are plaster drips here and there, including on his shoes, and a scuff of it on his pants. He chuckles when he sees me watching him. "Yes, it's hopeless," he says, "but I still try."

I can feel the cast start to lose its heat, and after a few more minutes Hank checks it, then unclamps the straps and says, "Ready?"

I nod, and after some gentle wiggling, the cast slides right off. He looks it over and smiles. "Beautiful."

Mom asks, "So how long does it take for you to make the socket?"

"Usually about a week." He looks from her to me, then says, "But how about I shoot for Friday?"

"That would be great," she says.

He nods. "We'll give you a call when it's ready."

I tie on my left shoe and gather my crutches, and on the way out I run into Chloe in the hallway. "Oh, excuse me!" she says, and dances out of my way.

We smile and say our goodbyes, and as I hobble out to the car on my crutches, I'm filled with a very strange feeling.

One I thought I might never feel again.

Hope.

chapter 3

I MISSED MATH ON MONDAY because of my appointment with Dr. Wells, and although Fiona got the homework for me, I had trouble with the lesson and don't want to miss another day of math if I can help it.

So after my fitting at Hank's, Mom and I go through the Taco Bell drive-through, and I gobble down lunch and get back to school in time for fifth and sixth periods.

I manage to catch Fiona up on the day's events during fifth, and I make her laugh, too, by calling it Hankenstein's lab.

"Wow," she says as she's walking with me over to the math wing, "Chloe sounds amazing."

"She is! If she hadn't knocked on her leg, I would never have known which one was fake."

So I hobble into math in a fine mood, and sit in a chair that I pull up next to Rosa. "I missed you yesterday!" she says. And as I'm watching her lips, working at decoding her words, she adds, "I was a little worried."

"I'm fine," I assure her, and I feel good that she missed me. So I start babbling about being fitted for a leg at Hankenstein's lab. She laughs too, and I'm really enjoying that I'm making people laugh instead of squirm or turn away. I'm also feeling good that Rosa missed me and was worried about me. Something about it is incredibly . . . sweet.

Then the tardy bell rings.

"Pass your homework all the way over," Ms. Rucker commands. She's looking even more stony-faced than usual, sizing up the class from behind her podium.

"*All* the way over?" somebody asks. "We're not grading them?"

"All the way," Ms. Rucker replies.

"Oh boy," I grumble, because my paper is incomplete.

Barely started is more accurate.

I'd planned to get help from Fiona, but . . . it hadn't happened. And I'd planned to "fill in the blanks" during the explanation, like a lot of people do . . . but there's no getting away with that now.

Ms. Rucker strolls toward us down the aisle, collecting papers as she approaches. I know better than to try to explain about going to Dr. Wells and getting my leg cast today. I know that in Ms. Rucker's eyes no excuse could validate such a miserable attempt at the homework.

Rosa sees my paper and her eyes grow wide. She passes hers to me and whispers something, but I can't understand it and I'm not in the right frame of mind to try.

Instinctively, I place her work on top of mine. The penmanship is jagged. Like her hands can't quite produce a smooth line. The numbers are a combination of miniature lightning bolts and uneven curves. But the work, the process, the steps . . . they're all tidy and easy to follow, with the answers clearly boxed.

Ms. Rucker takes the papers from me, inspecting them as she turns and walks toward the front of the classroom. It takes only three steps for her to stop and level a look at me over her shoulder.

The look lasts maybe two seconds, but in that time she manages to convey disappointment, doubt, and resentment. Here she let me slide on half the problems for all the days I was absent—why can't I show more effort?

I want to scream, Because I've missed a month of school, that's why! Because I just about died, that's why! Because everything I do is hard now, that's why!

Instead, my chin quivers and I turn away.

Rosa passes me a note. *I can help you after school.*

My mom's picking me up right after, I write back.

Way inside, though, I know this is an excuse.

The truth is, I'd rather have Fiona help me.

I can understand Fiona.

She's my friend.

She's . . . comfortable.

Rosa writes, *Call me if you want*, and jots down her phone number.

I smile and nod, and tuck away the note, then turn my attention to the board, where Ms. Rucker has begun the lesson.

It's hard to concentrate, though.

I sailed into class feeling sunny and hopeful, but now here I am.

Crashed against the rocks again.

chapter 4

THAT NIGHT I BURY MYSELF in my homework, but at bedtime I still don't feel like I've made a dent. There's so much reading to do. Especially in language and history. But what worries me most is math.

Especially the new assignments.

Today's math.

Yesterday's math.

They're adding up quickly to tomorrow's headache.

I try calling Fiona but can't reach her. First she's at track, then she's out with her mother, then she's busy with something else. At ten-thirty I give up and tell myself that I'll get her to help me in the morning.

But in the morning Fiona calls to say she overslept, and Mom barely gets me to school on time. There is absolutely no chance for Fiona to help me during the morning classes, and at lunch she rushes off to some meeting.

"Hey!" I call after her. "I really need help with math!"

"I'm sorry!" she calls back. "If I could get out of this, I would!"

She's gone, and I'm left leaning on my crutches not even knowing where she's going that's so important.

"Darn!" I grumble, and I'm feeling very frustrated as I hobble toward the courtyard to eat the lunch Mom packed me. I'm hating math, hating Ms. Rucker . . . plus I don't even know where I'm going to eat, or who I'm going to sit with. It's been ages since I've had lunch in the courtyard, and the closer I get to it, the more I do not want to go there. Especially without Fiona.

I'm also feeling really dumb about Rosa.

Why didn't I call her last night?

So I'm mad at Ms. Rucker, and mad at myself. And I'm hobbling by the 400 Wing when I remember—Rosa eats in Room 402.

I stop for a second, then turn and find the room. And when I peek through the door, there's Rosa in her wheelchair, laughing with two other girls in wheelchairs.

There are also two boys and a teacher in the classroom. The boys are working on an impressively large Lincoln Log house that's made out of pretzel sticks. The teacher's reading a book.

"Hey!" Rosa calls, beaming a bright smile my way.

I hobble in and sit in a chair near her. "I am so lost in math."

"I'll help you!" she says. Her voice sounds a little like voices do when you try to talk underwater, but now it's music to my ears.

"Oh, thank you," I say, and pull out the assignment.

First Rosa introduces me to her friends. "This is Leesha and Panny. . . . The guys are Illy and Twent."

I translate this to mean Alisha and Penny, Billy and Trent, but I'm not entirely sure.

"And I'm Mrs. Wahl," the teacher calls with a friendly wave. "You must be Jessica."

I nod and smile, but I feel a little uncomfortable that she already knows who I am.

Rosa gets right down to the math. She shows me her homework and points me through the steps as she explains the problems. "Okay. To find the first three iterates of this function, here's what you do. . . ."

I struggle to understand her, especially since she's speaking math—a language I'm already having trouble with. But seeing her work really helps, and at the end of each problem she forces me to get it by making me do the problem on my own without looking at her paper.

She's patient and encouraging, and every time I solve a problem right, she says, "See? You're getting it!" And as I begin solving them on my own, she smiles and says, "See? It's easy!"

And with her help, that's what it becomes.

Well, almost, anyway.

When the warning bell rings, I pack up my things and Rosa says, "I can help you anytime."

"Thanks," I say back, and this time I know that I'll take her up on it.

"I can come over, too," she says.

I hesitate, wondering how in the world that would work, or how she could even offer. It would probably be a lot easier for me to go over to her house . . . but again, my mind is defaulting to relying on Fiona for help.

Then she totally surprises me by saying, "I would love to meet your dog. He seems so . . . happy."

I blink at her. "How do you know my dog?" I'm feeling very strange. Not fully grounded. And it flashes through my mind that I've been stalked by a girl in a wheelchair.

She laughs at my expression. "You used to run by my house. I live on Marigold. The house with the mermaid fountain."

For some reason she's becoming easier to understand. I barely have to decipher at all. "I know that house! You're about half a mile from me. I'm on Harken."

"See?" she says with a lopsided smile as she motors toward the door. "We're neighbors."

Mrs. Wahl calls, "Bye, girls!" as we leave, and adds, "Come back anytime, Jessica. You're always welcome!"

"Thanks," I call back.

Then I hobble off to class.

chapter 5

THAT NIGHT I have the running dream again. When I wake up, I cry like I always do, but my tears are interrupted by the memory of something new in the dream.

A mermaid fountain.

A mermaid fountain and Rosa, waving from her porch as I run by.

In the dream I don't really see her. I don't turn my head and look. She's a ghost on the porch, a cloudy vapor to my right.

But I know she's there.

I know it's her.

I wonder about her appearing in the dream. The dream's been the same for so long, and this new dimension feels a little . . . invasive. This is *my* dream. My escape to the place I love most in the world. The roads, the river, the trees, the bridge . . .

Sherlock gives me a hopeful nudge and lets out a soft whine.

"Sorry, boy," I tell him. "After school we'll throw the ball, okay?"

He hasn't given up on our old routine but seems to like the new one just fine. I give him a hug and a nuzzle, and it crosses my mind that after I get my leg, I could walk him over to Rosa's.

The thought, in its own small way, makes me feel better.

chapter 6

THERE IS SOMETHING DIFFERENT about Fiona. Something... radiant. She denies it, but I don't believe her. "Are you in love?" I finally ask during science.

She assures me she's not.

"Then what is going on with you?" I whisper. "And don't tell me nothing!"

She finally caves, but only a little. "You'll see!"

"See what?" I demand, but she refuses to say any more.

So now I'm suspecting that it's not about her at all—that it's about me.

But what could it possibly be?

More cupcakes?

She leads me to Kyro's room at lunch. "Why?" I want to know. "What is going on?"

She's bursting at the seams. "Kyro has something *amazing* to show you!"

"What?" I demand.

"Stop asking! This is his surprise."

From the buildup I'm expecting a room full of people, but it's just Kyro.

Kyro and his laptop.

Kyro has ancestors from Poland and Ethiopia. He has dark skin and light eyes and the most beautiful hands I've ever seen. The fingers are long and graceful, and they do a little flip upward near the tips. But the overall impression is one of strength; that his hands could move mountains.

Kyro's hands are busy on the keys of his laptop when Fiona and I come in. "Jessica!" he says with a smile, then hits a few keys and turns to Fiona. "How much did you tell her?"

"Nothing!"

He grins. "I'm impressed."

"You should be!" she says with a laugh.

"Will one of you *please* tell me what this is about?"

He motions me over. "Have a seat."

So I sit in his seat and watch his computer screen as he activates a YouTube video.

It's footage of a track. A race. Some big event.

The commentator is speaking in a language I don't know. Italian?

"What is this?" I ask.

"Shhh," Kyro says. "Just watch."

There's a close-up now. A close-up of something I don't recognize. It's got little nails sticking out of a rubberized pad, and the pad is connected to a long, dark piece of curved metal.

And then the camera pulls back and I see that there are two of these spiky padded pieces of curved metal and that they're attached to . . . legs.

It's a runner?

Yes.

A runner on curved, spiked feet.

"That's Oscar Pistorius," Kyro says softly. "He's a four-hundred-meter sprinter, and a *double* below-knee amputee. Those are running prostheses."

"He *runs* on those?" I gasp, because it doesn't seem possible. His legs are sickles. Hooks. I don't understand how he can even stand on them, let alone run.

And yet he walks along the track, and then . . . he gets down in the starting blocks.

I hold my breath, not believing my eyes.

Kyro leans in and points out the other runners. "Look what he's competing against."

Every other runner getting into blocks has two legs.

Two flesh-and-blood legs.

The runners are set and the gun goes off, and the guy with hook legs fires out of the blocks just like the rest of the runners.

I watch, my heart pounding.

He can run!

He can *run*.

And not only can he run, he's *fast*. While other runners struggle through Rigor Mortis Bend, he gains ground, finishing the race in second place.

My jaw drops when the screen displays his time. "A forty-six nine?" I gasp.

Kyro grins. "Impressive, even on regular legs."

Kyro shows me two more videos—one with a woman

named Amy who's missing one leg below the knee just like me and runs *marathons*, and another with an amputee my age racing for her track team.

When they're done, he closes the laptop and looks right at me. "What do you think?"

"What do I *think*?" Thoughts race through my head.

It's amazing.

Unbelievable.

And freakish.

These people look like *cyborgs*.

Since I lost my leg, I've wanted to cover up. Hide what I'm missing. Make others forget there's something different about me.

There'd be no covering that up.

Is running worth becoming a cyborg?

Kyro gently prods me for an answer. "What I'm asking is would you want one?"

My heart races at the thought of being able to run again, and my moment of doubt vanishes.

"Yes!"

He nods. "Okay, then, here's the situation: Running prostheses are expensive. We already have plenty of problems with insurance companies covering your basic medical issues, but even if we didn't, getting them to pay for one of these is almost certainly out of the question. So we had a team meeting yesterday and formed the Help Jessica Run campaign. Every runner volunteered for at least one of four committees: Bake Sale, Raffle, Car Wash, and Community Donations." He takes a deep breath. "Our goal is to buy you a running leg so you can get back on the track and compete on the team your senior year."

I look from Kyro to Fiona and back again.

I want to say something, but what can I possibly say?

There are no words for this moment.

And I'm almost afraid to believe that I actually might be able to run again.

chapter 7

AT HOME I'M STILL HAVING TROUBLE believing it's true.

I'm going to be able to run again?

I watch the YouTube videos on our computer over and over, and slowly it sinks in.

I'm going to be able to run again!

I make my mother watch them.

She's amazed. "I have never seen anything like that!"

I make my sister watch them.

She's . . . direct. "That is *freaky*," she says after seeing the clips.

"It's *awesome*," I tell her, and give her a playful shove.

She wants to watch them again, and when we're done, she says, "You're really going to get one of those?"

"My team is doing this huge fund-raiser and they're going to buy me one! They're doing bake sales and raffle tickets and car washes. . . ."

"Seriously?" Kaylee asks.

"Seriously."

My dad, however, is secretly not convinced. I hear him in

the kitchen later, talking to my mom. "How are cookies and raffle tickets going to raise twenty thousand dollars?"

I hold my breath, eavesdropping from around the corner.

Twenty thousand dollars?!

For a curved piece of metal?

The team will never be able to raise that much money!

"Don't give her doubts," my mom whispers sternly. "She's happy. She's hopeful. She *needs* this."

My dad's voice is hoarse as he whispers, "But if it's a pipe dream, it's cruel! And what about the hospital bills and the twenty thousand for her regular prosthesis? Does he have any idea what we're going through to cover *those* bills?"

I hold my breath harder.

Twenty thousand?

Twenty thousand?

My mind is reeling.

If a leg costs that much, what did the hospital cost? For that matter, what did it cost to cut off my real leg?

"Look," my mom whispers. "Let's hire that lawyer and let's apply pressure. But let's not say anything negative about the team's plan to raise money. They're just trying to help."

"The lawyer wants half of whatever settlement we reach, and it might take years!"

"So let's interview another lawyer. And if they tell you the same thing, well, half of something is better than half of what we've got right now."

My dad sighs, and I can feel the tiredness that he seems to carry around everywhere. "Why can't they just step up to their responsibilities? Haven't we been put through enough?"

The kitchen falls silent, and even though it's hard to hop quietly, I do my best to hurry away without being found out.

And I do get away, but I can't escape the guilt.

Maybe the team's money should go to pay my medical bills.

Or pay for my regular leg.

Maybe there really are more important things than running.

I feel like such a burden.

Is it fair to even hope?

chapter 8

FIONA PICKS ME UP FOR SCHOOL the next morning, and she's a little chatterbox, which I find exhausting. Especially since it feels like I didn't sleep a wink the whole night. "They cost twenty thousand dollars!" I finally blurt. "Twenty *thousand* dollars!"

She pulls into the student parking lot. "What do?"

"Those running legs. I looked it up online."

She shrugs. "So we'll raise twenty thousand dollars."

I blink at her for a full minute, then shake my head and slouch in my seat. "You're dreaming."

She just smiles at me and starts chattering about something else.

First and second periods seem to drag on forever, and at break I seriously consider going home "sick." But I've already missed way too much school, so I tough it out, convincing myself that it's important to stay.

At lunch Fiona decides we should eat in the courtyard. "It's gorgeous out today! Who wants to be inside?" She parks me on a bench near a scrawny elm tree, where I feel strangely invisible as she goes off to fetch two mandarin chicken salads. Everyone seems to have somewhere to go, someone to see. It's not that people are trying not to look at me—they're just into their own things. It feels like I'm in a movie where everyone has a role and a place and a purpose, and I'm one of those silent extras they pay to sit and look like they're part of the show.

I'm relieved when Fiona returns. "Sorry that took so long!" she says, handing over my salad. She checks me over. "You doing okay?"

I shrug. "I don't know. I was so up yesterday, but I've definitely crashed back to earth today." I snap open the salad lid and sigh. "It's nice of the team to want to help, but do you remember how long it took to raise two thousand dollars for a new discus cage? It was almost two years! How are we ever going to raise *twenty* thousand?"

"Look," she says, zigzagging dressing across her salad, "you are not a discus cage. You are a flesh-and-blood person who this tragic thing has happened to. People will *want* to help." She smiles at me. "Give them a chance."

This should make me feel better, but it doesn't. A dark cloud has formed between me and the dream of running again.

A dark cloud called reality.

chapter 9

I HAVE A SOCKET FITTING scheduled at Hank's after school.

A socket fitting.

I don't really even know what that means.

I'm quiet on the drive over, and so is Mom. I wonder what's going on with her and Dad and the whole money issue, but I don't ask.

I just watch the road ahead.

So does she.

The exterior of Quality Orthotics and Prosthetics does nothing to lift my mood, but the instant we go inside, Chloe certainly does.

"Jessica!" she says from behind the counter. "Are you excited?"

I can't help but smile, because *she* sure seems to be. "I guess," I tell her.

"Well, come on back—he's ready for you."

My mom and I exchange looks as we follow Chloe—no Mr. Benson holding us up this time.

Chloe leads us to the same room we were in before, and

Hank comes in holding a clear plastic version of the cast he took on Tuesday. My name and the date are written right on it in black marker, and along the back are two screws holding the plastic together.

He greets us, then has me roll up my pant leg and take off my shrinker sock while he gets a stockingette out of a cupboard. After the stockingette is on, he holds up the plastic cast and says, "So this is your test socket. What we'll do today is check for pressure points, distribution of weight bearing, and fit. If there's anywhere that hurts, be sure to tell me. It should feel snug, and there'll be pressure, but after you get used to that, it shouldn't hurt." He smiles at me. "Ready?"

I nod, and he gets down on his knees and slips the socket over my stump.

I feel like a freak-show Cinderella, getting a strange glass slipper put on, but that image vanishes when I realize that the socket feels . . . good.

"How is that?" he asks.

"Surprisingly comfortable," I tell him.

He pushes up on it from the bottom. "How's that?"

"Okay," I tell him.

He pushes harder. "No pain?"

I shake my head.

"The clearance here," he says, pointing to the base of the socket, "should be enough so that you don't feel it when the leg is complete and you're standing on it, but not so much that it creates an area where your residual limb can pool with fluids." He nods. "I think we've got a good fit here."

Next he has me bend my knee, and he checks all around

it, especially in back. The kneecap is exposed, and the socket is cut away so I can flex, but it does pinch a little behind the knee.

"Does this need to come down some?" he asks.

"I think so."

He goes on to check the socket from all angles, making small marks on the plastic as we go over the pressure points. Then he has me stand and lean my short leg on a big block of wood.

It's the first time I've stood on both legs since the accident.

"How is that?"

"Very strange," I tell him.

"But is there pain? Excessive pressure? Close your eyes and feel it."

"Maybe a little right here," I tell him, pointing to a spot on the inside of my knee.

He marks it, and when he's sure there are no other spots, he has me sit down again and slips off the socket.

"I think we're set. I should have your leg ready a week from today. It will be a temporary prosthesis, Jessica, because your leg is still changing. But after you're trained on the temporary and your residual limb has had a few months to stabilize, we'll do this again, only with parts that are more suited for your lifestyle."

"Meaning?"

He looks at me. "You're an active young lady. We want to get you a leg that can keep up with you. But first things first, and that is to get you walking."

I'm about to ask him what he knows about running legs, but before I can, my mom says, "Could I have a word with you about . . . administrative matters?"

He glances from her to me and catches her drift. "Sure. Why don't we talk in my office?"

So they leave while I pull my shrinker sock back on and pin my pant leg up.

I try not to think about what "administrative matters" might be, because it's clearly about money.

I try to block the thought of running from my mind.

I try to focus on walking.

In one week I'll have a leg.

In one week I'll learn to walk again.

In one week.

chapter 10

IT TURNS OUT TO BE A LONG WEEK.

Not because I can't wait to get my leg. I am looking forward to that, but it also scares me a little. What if it's awful? What if I can't figure it out? What if it falls off during school?

No, it's a long week because the track team officially invites me to the meet on Thursday, and I'm terrified of going.

But how can I not?

Already the bake sales and the raffle ticket sales have started. Saturday will be the first Help Jessica Run car wash.

On the outside I'm grateful and happy, but inside I know it's an impossible goal.

They will never raise twenty thousand dollars.

People tell me all the time that I'm still part of the team. They're all excited to be buying me a leg. They're so nice. So positive.

They seem to have no idea what a pipe dream this is.

When Thursday arrives, I'm still not ready. But it's Liberty versus Langston—our main rival—and it's on our turf.

No busses to get on or traveling to do. All I have to do is hobble over to the track.

So easy.

And yet so hard.

I haven't even seen the track since I've been back at school. Not that it's been difficult to avoid. It's out past the gym and the locker rooms, past the basketball courts and the tennis courts and the baseball diamonds. It's the last school structure before empty fields, and it sits on a small rise of land unprotected from the afternoon winds.

Jocks snicker at runners. They think it doesn't take much skill to put one foot in front of the other; that anyone can run track. And I guess people like Merryl Abrams contribute to that, but those of us who are serious about it grin and bear a lot more than players in some "real" sports.

Basketball players wouldn't dream of doing wind sprints in the rain.

Tennis players call off practice if the courts are even a little wet.

Volleyball players won't have anything to do with the cold.

And football players? They chalk talk or pump iron when the weather gets wicked.

It's the soccer players and the track teams that show all-weather grit. And at Liberty High the track teams are the only ones of *any* of the sports to ever win league. And the varsity girls are contenders almost every year.

People don't understand why we run. It seems so mindless to them. All you do is go around and around the track.

That's the funny thing about running. The deceptive thing about it. It may seem mindless, but it's really largely mental. If the mind's not strong, the body acts weak, even if it's not. If the mind says it's too cold or too rainy or too windy to run, the body will be more than happy to agree. If the mind says it would be better to rest or recover or cut practice, the body will be glad to oblige.

My mother says I was born a runner; that I entered this world wanting to get up and *go*. Kaylee, on the other hand, has always hated running. Not because I love it, but simply because she hates it. She tried it a couple of summers ago, but after a week of easy jogs with me, she asked, "When do you stop counting your steps?"

I didn't know how to answer that.

I'd never counted steps in my life.

So maybe it's something you're born with. Or maybe it's something you adopt. I just know that for me, running was like eating and breathing—it was something I had always done, and without it I felt miserable.

Suffocated.

Losing a leg was like having to learn to suck in air through the pores of my skin.

Somehow I survived, but each breath was painful.

And then Kyro showed me the footage of amputees running.

And running *fast*.

Air seemed to fill my lungs again. I was heady and happy and I could feel myself—a future me—running.

I want to hold on to that.

I want to believe.

But twenty thousand dollars of reality has sunk in, and my lungs have shut down again. I feel like I'm trapped under a layer of ice, holding on to what little air I have, drowning under a cold, hard ceiling that's keeping me from something that can save me.

chapter 11

AFTER SCHOOL, Shandall Norwood catches me teetering with uncertainty near the tennis courts. "Hey, girl!" she calls, and zips over. "Why you standing out here?"

I shrug. "I was going to go to the meet to cheer you guys on, but . . ."

My voice trails off, so she finishes for me. "But you're not sure you can handle it?" Her words come out gentle. Like she totally gets it.

My throat closes down and my eyes fill up.

"Aw, girl," she says, putting her arm around me. "We're gonna get you running again, you know that."

I shrug.

"Look, if you can't handle going to the meet, don't come. Everyone'll understand."

"But it's *Langston*."

She understands this too. Langston's got state-of-the-art everything. From their starting blocks to their jumping standards to their landing systems and cages and hurdles and *bleachers*, their equipment totally puts Liberty High to shame.

It's their track, though, that has us all green with envy.

Ours is dirt.

Theirs is a Tartan track.

It's the most amazing track I've ever run on. It's clean, smooth, and *fast*, and it's a beautiful royal blue. Whenever I race at Langston, I imagine that I'm running across water. It's an incredible feeling.

So Langston is our big league rival, and even though they have everything our team would love to have, we have the one thing a team can't buy.

Spirit.

Maybe it's a bond formed from years of running into the wind. Maybe it's because Kyro calls us his family and expects us to treat one another that way. Maybe it's just the fight of the underdog. Whatever it is, we have it, and Langston doesn't. Oh, they *act* like they do, but you can feel it—it's just a show.

Shandall studies me, and very slyly she says, "Yeah, that Vanessa Steele's gonna be prancin' all over the place like she's unbeatable or somethin'. Like you never even existed."

Blood prickles through my body.

Vanessa Steele.

She refused to shake my hand after I beat her at the West-field Invitational.

She's probably relieved that I've been knocked out of the competition.

I clench my crutches and start in the direction of the track. "Let's go," I tell Shandall.

"Thatta girl," she says, and falls into step beside me.

We talk about her events, and I kid her a little about her discus release. Then, when we're near the track, I stop for a moment and soak in the view. The starter's already there and easy to spot in his red hat and coat, and the Langston teams are trudging through a warm-up lap. Our teams are scattered, warming up in groups, helping Kyro deliver things to the various officials and field judges. There's JV girls, JV boys, varsity girls, varsity boys—four teams from each school is a lot to coordinate.

"There it is," Shandall says with mock reverence. "The Oval of Pain."

I laugh and tell her, "Go on. You've got to warm up, stretch out, and bring home some fives!"

"I don't know about *that*," she says, "but if I get a third and we win by one, I'm takin' credit for the whole shootin' match!"

"You do that!" I laugh.

She takes off, and I swing forward toward the field.

I want to wish my team good luck.

And I want to stand among them and somehow believe that I still belong.

chapter 12

I JOIN THE PRE-MEET LIBERTY HUDDLE, then stay infield to cheer on runners in the 4×100–meter relays and the 1600-meter runs. The heats go fast—JV girls, JV boys, varsity girls, varsity boys—but each race is still a long process.

When the varsity girls line up for the 1600, I head over to Rigor Mortis Bend and shout my heart out for Fiona each time she goes by. She's ahead at the 800-meter mark, but I can see her tighten up during the third lap. She holds on for as long as she can, but at 1400 meters she loses her lead and has to fight with everything she's got to stay in second place.

She does get second, though, which brings in three points for the team, but she is not happy. "That's six seconds slower than my PR," she says, gasping for air when we meet up. "That third lap *killed* me. I just never recovered."

I give her a pep talk and a hug, and after she's caught her breath, she mutters, "Time to play nice with the Manipulator," and wanders off to the high-jump pit.

I don't tag along. I'm feeling kind of worn out, and I'm really not in the mood to make phony chitchat with Merryl

Abrams. Especially since it's pretty hard not to notice that Gavin's over there with her. So when Kyro and some parent helpers start setting up hurdles, I take the opportunity to crutch across the track to the bleachers.

Liberty High's track has only one set of bleachers. It's got steps up the middle, which divides it into two sections, one for home, one for away. Nobody pays attention to that, though. Even with our standing in league, usually the only people who show up at track meets are dedicated parents, plus the occasional boyfriend or girlfriend. It's not like there are squads of cheering voices. Besides, it's way more important to find a group to huddle with to help body-block the rising winds, and some afternoons anyone will do.

As I hobble across the track, I feel like I'm getting stares from people in the bleachers. I can see parents whispering to each other about me.

Or maybe I'm imagining it.

Maybe they're not noticing me at all.

I go up the entrance steps, take a seat on the bottom bench, lay my crutches down, and unload my backpack. Then I sit through the 100-meter hurdles for the girls and the 110-meter high hurdles for the boys.

There are legs, legs, everywhere.

I watch them move so effortlessly.

Pair after pair of perfectly tuned, beautifully timed legs.

How could I never have seen them this way before?

In between the races I watch the high-jump pit, out in the distance.

Gavin's still there.

I feel my heartbeat grow faster inside my chest. I try to calm it, but it pounds maddeningly harder. Pretty soon, my breathing turns shallow, and then there's the familiar flutter of butterflies in my stomach.

This has nothing to do with Gavin Vance.

It has everything to do with the hurdles being cleared.

The 400-meter is next.

Starting blocks are adjusted, and soon the JV girls shake out and get into position.

I grip the rail in front of me as the starter calls, "To your mark! Set!" Then the starting gun cracks and my heart gallops away.

I want to cheer for the girls. I want to dash to the infield and root them around Rigor Mortis Bend. But all I can do is death-grip the rail and fight back the lump in my throat.

This is not my heat, but this is my race.

My race.

There's a soft voice beside me. "Jessica?"

I turn and see a woman I don't know sitting beside me.

Oh, wait. She *is* a little familiar.

My mind scrambles to remember. She's not one of our runners' moms. She's actually too well put together for any kind of track mom. Her hair's long and sleek with subtle highlights. Her hands are perfectly manicured. But mostly it's her clothes—they're classy. Nothing sweats-like about them.

Who is she?

"I'm Claudia Steele," she says softly. "Vanessa's mom?"

She has her hand out, so I shake it, but I'm stunned.

"I just want to say how sorry I am," she begins.

I move to pull my hand away, but she holds it.

"I don't know the right words to use," she continues. "I don't know if there are right words."

In her eyes I see . . . sincerity.

My hand stops pulling.

"Thanks," I tell her, and for a moment I forget that there's a race going on.

She does finally let go of my hand, but she doesn't leave. Through the JV boys' race neither of us says a word. And it's odd to sit through the girls' varsity lineup with her beside me.

I wish her away. Her being there is making me terribly uncomfortable. But she just sits there, silently watching as Vanessa adjusts her trademark racing glasses, rolls her shoulders and neck, shakes out her legs, and finally gets down in the blocks.

"This has to be very hard on you," Mrs. Steele says.

I keep my eyes fixed on the runners. *Please*, I think, *just go away*. But then out of my mouth slips, "This is my first time back."

I could kick myself.

Why am I talking to her if I want her to go away?

The gun goes off and Vanessa shoots from the blocks. She gathers speed and her stride lengthens. Her legs are long.

Fluid.

Beautiful.

I close my eyes and try to stop my chin from quivering.

What made me think I could do this?

Vanessa wins the race easily, which gives Langston five

points. But we get three for second and one for third, so Langston nets only one point.

Still, it's hard to take.

Especially with my rival's mother sitting beside me.

I'm just thinking of an excuse to leave, since she's not, when Vanessa comes clomping up the steps. She's still wearing her racing glasses. "That track is a *joke*," she spits out. "This whole place is a joke! My time was terrible!"

I have an urge to flatten her.

She's made her mother uncomfortable too. And I can tell Mrs. Steele wants to say something to her daughter, but before she can, Vanessa holds out a hand. "Can I see my phone?"

Her mother produces it from her purse, and as she's handing it over, she says, "You recognize Jessica Carlisle, don't you?"

"Yeah, hey," she says to me, checking for texts. She hands the phone back to her mother, then turns and walks away.

"Vanessa!" her mother calls, but Vanessa says, "I've got to get a rubdown before the hurdles!"

"Vanessa!" her mother snaps, but she doesn't even get acknowledged this time.

"Excuse my daughter," Mrs. Steele says after a moment. Her hands are shaking as she refastens her purse, and when it's closed, she faces me and says, "No, excuse *me* for raising such a self-absorbed daughter."

Then she stands and walks away, leaving me the same way she found me.

Stunned.

chapter 13

AFTER I GET OVER MY SHOCK, I can only think of one thing to do.

Tell Fiona!

I wait until the next race is over, then crutch across the track and make my way toward the high-jump area.

Before I can reach it, Gavin intercepts me. "It's great to see you out here!" he says.

It's the first time I've seen him at any meet ever, so I tell him, "It's great to see you out here, too," but with limited enthusiasm. I nod over at Merryl, who's a few yards away, pulling on her sweats. "How'd she do?"

He glances over his shoulder at her. "She tried her best."

I hold back a snicker, because he seems to really mean it. Merryl's best is about 4'6" and involves a lot of drama. And since high jump is her only event, she's always finding some excuse to leave after she's eliminated. "So you taking off?" I ask.

"Are you kidding? This is Langston! We're the underdogs! We need to win this thing!"

I give him a curious look. "Wow, Gavin. I had no idea you were so into track."

He laughs. "It's sort of contagious, isn't it?" There's a sweetness to the blush of his cheeks that I try very hard to ignore.

"You ever thought about running?"

He shrugs. "I used to be fast in elementary school . . . but that was a long time ago. And I don't exactly come from a family of sportspeople."

I eye him. "You can be a politician *and* run, you know. And I'm not talking about for office."

He laughs again, then gives his chin scruff a thoughtful scratch. "That's a whole new paradigm, isn't it?"

Merryl is suddenly upon us. "Hey, Jess," she says, then turns to Gavin. "I have a killer headache. I really need to get home."

This creates an awkward moment, so I tell them both, "See ya," and hobble over in time to see Fiona's approach. The bar's at 4'10", and she flips over it with ease.

"Nice!" I tell her when she comes back around. They have to cycle through all the remaining jumpers before it's Fiona's turn again, so I've got time to tell her what happened. "Guess who sat next to me during the four hundred."

"Who?"

"Vanessa Steele's *mother*."

"No!" She blinks at me. "On purpose?"

So I tell her the story from beginning to end, and when I'm done, she gasps, "Unbelievable! The whole thing is unbelievable!"

"Bartlett!" the pit judge calls. "Bartlett, you're up!"

"Gotta go," Fiona says. She takes her mark, composes herself, rocks back and forth a few times, then approaches the bar and flips right over it.

She returns to me, breathless. "I am so pumped right now!" she laughs. "Everyone will be when they hear about it!"

I grab her arm. "Wait! No! You can't tell other people!"

"Why not?" she asks, incredulous.

"Because . . ." I try to sort things out quickly in my mind, but I don't really know why. It just feels wrong. "Because her mom was really nice."

"So?"

"So . . . I think it's . . . you know . . . bad karma."

She squints at me. "Bad *karma*? Vanessa Steele is what's bad karma!"

"Look, just don't, okay?"

She sighs. "Whatever you say." Then she gets fiery again. "But I'm gonna yell my lungs out for Annie and Giszelda in the three-hundred hurdles."

"I'll yell with you!" I say it with a laugh, because we always cheer for them. Annie and Giszelda are fun and funny, and awesome hurdlers.

They're just not as good as Vanessa.

chapter 14

IT'S DOWN TO TWO VARSITY GIRL high jumpers—Fiona and a Langston jumper named Yassi—when the hurdles are set up again for the 300-meter race. The finish line is very near the high-jump area, which is pretty convenient for us, but it's doing nothing for Fiona's concentration. She already missed one pass at 5'2" when the JV girls were hurdling, and when we see varsity line up, she decides she doesn't want to risk missing again.

"I'll be back in a minute!" she tells the pit judge after Yassi has a second miss.

"Wait!" the judge says. "Can't you finish your jumps?"

"Give me *two* minutes!" she begs, and when he nods, we hurry toward the 200-meter mark as fast as I can.

Across the field, Vanessa is making a show of getting into her blocks, running through her psych-out routine.

I try telepathing my mantra over to Annie and Giszelda.

Smooth, strong, fast. Smooth, strong, fast.

I think it hard, trying to cancel Vanessa's psych-out.

The gun goes off and the girls shoot forward, finding their stride, leaping over the first hurdle, regaining their stride, leaping over the second hurdle.

It makes no sense to cheer from so far away, so instead Fiona grumbles, "Who does she think she is, always wearing those glasses?"

"C'mon, Annie," I'm starting to call. Annie's still too far away to hear me, but I can't help it. "C'mon, Annie!"

They round the bend, and Vanessa's lead is becoming clear. She's in lane two, with Annie on her right shoulder and Giszelda on her left.

"Catch her, Annie! You can do it!" I shout, and I find myself hopping up and down on my leg.

The sound of their pounding is getting louder.

Like a stampede.

"GO, ANNIE!" I shout. "YOU CAN CATCH HER!"

And then, only a few yards away from us, the unthinkable happens.

Vanessa's foot catches on her hurdle.

Suddenly she's flailing through the air.

The hurdle crashes forward, and although it almost takes Annie out, somehow Annie maneuvers around it and stays in her lane. Giszelda nearly wipes out avoiding Vanessa, but she manages to stay in her lane, too.

In the time it takes to gasp, the race is over, and to everyone's shock, Liberty has swept the event.

Vanessa is back on her feet and she is *furious*.

"Well, I guess *she's* okay," Fiona says with a snort. "Man, listen to her!"

"Wouldn't want her mad at me," I laugh, and we join our winning girls in pogoing around.

"Bartlett!" the pit judge hollers.

Fiona zips back to the high jump and wins the event by clearing 5'3". And she is so psyched by everything that's happened that she has the bar raised to 5'4½" and sets a new PR.

Then Kyro appears, and although he's congratulatory toward Fiona, I can tell that something's wrong.

"What's going on?" I ask him.

His lips pinch together for a moment, and then he says, "Langston has lodged a complaint with the red-hat. Vanessa Steele believes that you were planted on the sidelines to distract her."

This takes a minute to sink in.

"What?" I ask.

"What?" Fiona asks.

"What?" everyone around us demands.

Kyro lets out a heavy sigh. "I know. But I need to ask—what were you shouting from the sidelines?"

"What was I shouting?" I give him an incredulous look. "I don't know. 'Go, Annie, go'? Something like that?"

"You weren't yelling *at* her?" he asks.

"No!" I look to Fiona for support, and she jumps in with "Absolutely not! She was rooting for Annie."

Kyro takes a deep breath. "Okay, then. The red-hat called it a ridiculous charge, but I want to set the record straight regardless. I'll have a talk with him and the coach."

"Do you want me to come?" I ask.

He hesitates, then says, "You know, that might be a good idea."

So I crutch across the field. And in the meeting with the starter and Langston's coach I explain that I was just rooting for my team like everyone else does.

While I'm talking, I can see Vanessa in the background pacing back and forth. Her mother is trying to talk to her, but Vanessa is obviously more interested in watching us than listening to her.

Finally I say, "Look, can you just call Vanessa over? I'll apologize, even though I really don't see how her clipping a hurdle was my fault."

The Langston coach waves Vanessa over, and with her mother's nudging she joins us. She's still got her sunglasses on, so it's hard to make eye contact with her, but I look straight at the lenses and say, "Hey, Vanessa. I was just cheering on my own team—I'm sorry if I was a distraction to you."

She doesn't say a thing.

I give a little shrug and chuckle, and I try to make light of it. "I guess I'm probably a distraction to everybody, huh?"

A heartbeat passes.

That's all.

Then she turns to the starter and says, "So why is she here? If she knows she's a distraction to everyone, why is she here?"

I feel my body flush hot.

Kyro steps forward. "Because she's still part of our team, that's why."

It's obvious that Vanessa is thinking, *Oh, right,* and that's when it sinks in.

I'm not really part of the team.

Not anymore.

My eyes burn as I hurry away.

It was a nice fantasy, but that's all it was.

chapter 15

I'M STILL IN A COMPLETE FUNK the next day, and in no mood for icy Ms. Rucker.

"Jessica," she says after the tardy bell rings, "when are you planning to return to your regular seat?"

It's true that I'm moving around on my crutches much better than I used to.

It's true that the reason she sat me back with Rosa was because I was in a wheelchair.

It's true that other people with crutches just sit in their regular seats.

And I *am* getting my leg today.

But days ago, I decided—I'm staying at Rosa's table. Even when I'm walking again, I'm staying.

"I'm not," I tell her, and I'm surprised by the sound of my own voice.

It's confident.

With a twinge of defiance.

Ms. Rucker holds my gaze. "I think it might be better for Rosa if you took your assigned seat."

"No!" Rosa says, and everyone turns to look at her. "I like her here," Rosa says in her underwatery tones. "Please."

Ms. Rucker frowns, then looks from me to Rosa and back again. "Then the note writing has got to stop."

I look at Rosa.

Rosa looks at me.

Our faces both say Oops!

"Fine," I say to Ms. Rucker. "But she's just been helping me keep up. Rosa's a math genius, you know."

Ms. Rucker studies me. "Yes, I'm aware of that," she says, and decides not to argue with me about the content of our notes, even though she knows I'm fibbing. "Math lab would be a more constructive option," she says with one eyebrow arched high. Then she begins writing on the board.

Rosa immediately slips me a note.

Thanks.

I smile at her. And for the first time since the track meet, I smile inside, too.

chapter 16

MOM NOTICES HOW QUIET I AM as she drives me to Hank's. "Are you okay?"

I nod but say, "I don't understand how this fake leg is going to work. What if I can't *make* it work?"

"You'll figure it out, sweetheart. Remember Chloe, okay? We couldn't even tell."

That does help. And Chloe's her usual bubbly self when she sees us, which helps too. "Today's the day!" she says as we check in. "Did you bring shorts and your right shoe?"

I nod and hold them up. "Can I change? We came straight from school."

She leads me to a small bathroom, and on the way she says, "It'll feel weird at first, but don't be discouraged. I know you'll get the hang of it fast, and once you do, you'll be walking everywhere!" She says it quietly. Conspiratorially. Like she's sharing a secret.

Like we're friends.

She takes my right running shoe from me. "You'll definitely use a cane or a crutch at first, but you'll get rid of that in no time too."

"Thanks," I tell her, and I'm grateful to hear this from someone who knows.

Someone I believe.

After I've changed into shorts, Chloe waves me down to a room with mirrored walls and long parallel bars. The bars are at about hip height and maybe three feet apart. It looks remotely like a dance studio, only instead of tutus there are miscellaneous fake body parts here and there, and the only "dancers" are Hank and my mother.

Their conversation stops immediately when I walk in. Hank picks up a fake leg from against the wall and smiles at me. "Time to get you walking again!"

It looks like a mannequin's foot with a metal pipe sticking out of it. The pipe is about eight inches long and an inch and a half in diameter, with two metal connectors—one down by the foot, and one up where the pipe attaches to the socket. The connectors have little holes and divots in them and look like strange plumbing couplings—like something my dad might use under a sink.

On top of the pole is the finished socket. It's skin-colored and is cut away at the knee so it looks like a kind of stirrup for my leg.

He grins at me as I soak it all in. "Yes, it's a little Hankensteinish, but—"

My focus snaps to my mom. "You *told* him?"

She looks chagrined, but he says, "I laughed my head off, Jessica. I might even change the name of my business to Hankenstein's, but unfortunately, most of my clients aren't in the frame of mind for such humor." He eyes me. "It's a really good sign that you are."

I'm still embarrassed, but I nod and say, "So what do I do?"

He has me take off my left shoe and sit in a chair that's right by the parallel bars. Then he hands me a tube-shaped nylon to put over my stump, and has me put a "stump sock" on over the nylon—it's like a regular sock only with no heel shape or seam. It's also softer and stretchier than a regular sock.

"Now for the liner," he says, and pulls a white foamy-looking thing out of the socket of my fake leg. He hands over the liner and says, "Just slip this on and tell me how it feels."

"Is it supposed to be snug?" I ask. "It feels a little loose."

He takes it off and has me put on a thicker-ply sock, then put the liner on again.

This time it seems to fit better, so he holds the fake leg so that the open end of the socket is facing my stump and says, "Just put your leg inside."

I do, and it's a snug, comfortable fit. But it's very strange to look down and see a pipe leg and a fake foot attached to me. "How does it stay on?" I ask, because it sure doesn't seem like I could actually *walk* with it.

"We'll get to that in a minute. First I want to check the fit." He pushes and twists the socket, and when he's sure it's okay, he pulls the leg off and says, "We're going to use a suspension sleeve to hold the leg in place." He picks up a tan rubbery-looking sleeve and starts pulling it onto the outside of the socket. "This is a neoprene material, like what wet suits are made of. The sleeve will create a vacuum between you and your prosthetic leg that will hold it firmly in place." He doubles the sleeve back over the socket, then holds the leg out for me. "If I can get you to slip your leg in?"

So I do, and then he has me pull the doubled-back part of the sleeve up over my leg. It's like a big, rubbery sock that ends about mid-thigh and seems to suck the fake leg on tight.

"Ready to stand?" he asks.

"I guess so," I answer, but then I just sit there, frozen in place.

"Use the bars if you want to. Just stand like you remember doing."

It's strange. It's like my brain doesn't quite remember what it used to do. I've been hopping and crutching for so long, getting up and down differently . . . I'm almost afraid to try.

So I grab the bars and I use my left leg to power myself up.

"Put weight on it," he encourages me. "It shouldn't hurt."

But I'm not so much afraid of the pain as I am of not being able to work this pipe leg.

I get a rush of panic—how is this ever going to work?

How am I ever going to be able to walk on this thing?

Slowly, I put weight on my right leg. It takes a minute for my leg to settle in, and when it does, I feel lopsided. Like my fake leg is way too long.

"Is your weight distributed evenly?" Hank asks. When I nod, he says, "I'm going to check the height now," and puts his thumbs on the crest points of my hip bones.

"The leg feels way too long," I tell him.

He nods knowingly. "That's normal. You've had no resistance or pressure on that leg for quite some time now, so even when it's perfect, patients still say it feels long." He smiles at me. "But in this case, it *is* long."

He takes a thin wooden block and slips it under my good

foot, then checks my hip bones again. "By raising the left side," he says, "I'll know how much I have to shorten the pylon." After a minute of assessing how level I am, he takes another, thinner block and slips it under my left foot so that it's on top of the first block.

"Very good," he says after checking the level again. "The first block was half an inch, the second one a quarter inch . . . which means we've got to take the pylon down three-quarters of an inch."

He has me sit down and uses an Allen wrench to loosen the top coupling. Then he removes the pipe from the socket. The foot is still attached to the bottom end of the pipe, and having him do this feels strange. Like I'm some sort of doll where the parts snap on and off.

He leaves the room with the pipe and foot, and before long he's back. "Let's try this," he says, and reattaches the pipe to the socket.

I stand up again, and even though the leg still feels long, he checks the level and says, "Perfect."

"Are you sure?" I ask.

"I am. Don't worry. That feeling of it being too long will go away." Then he says, "Now what I want you to do is hold on to the bars and just rock back and forth on one foot, then the other."

I do this, and what's so surreal is that I can feel my foot. It's not there, I know it's not there, but as I'm rocking back and forth, my brain seems to be sighing with relief.

Oh, there it is!

"How is that?" Hank asks.

"Is it supposed to feel like my foot is there?" I ask quietly.

"Does it?" he asks in return.

I nod, then look at him.

He's smiling. "It's not the case for everyone, that's for sure. But I find that the patients who have that sensation adapt much more quickly than those who don't."

"But why does it feel that way?"

"Your brain is still wired to your having a foot." He shrugs. "The body's nerves send signals, and the brain adapts or reacts. That can be a phantom pain or simply feeling like a limb is still there. It's not entirely understood, but if your brain thinks your prosthetic foot is your real foot, that's a very good sign."

I glance at my mother, and she's looking a little tense, but also . . . pleased.

"All right," Hank says. "Now I want you to put your left foot forward, then pull it back. Put your right foot forward, pull it back. Don't go anywhere, just do a little hokey-pokey for me."

So I do, and each time I put my right leg out and back, I feel a little more confident.

"Let's try a few steps," he says when I've hokey-pokeyed enough. "Hold on to the rails and move forward. The biggest obstacle is fear, and you have no reason to be afraid. Just do what your body remembers."

And so I take my first step.

And my second step.

And my third.

The fake leg feels snug.

Solid.

I can't roll off the foot like I can with my regular leg, but I move forward step by step until suddenly I'm at the end of the bars.

I look up and see my reflection in the mirror.

My new leg is not a pretty sight, but it doesn't freak me out.

I turn around, and there's my mother and Hank, standing at the opposite end.

My mother has a look on her face that's hard to define. Hope. Anticipation. Worry . . . I feel like I'm her baby again, taking my first wobbly steps.

I take a deep breath, then loosen my grip on the bars.

Two steps forward, my hands are hovering above the bars.

I take two more steps.

And two more.

Tears sting my eyes.

I'm *walking*.

chapter 17

IT'S ALMOST ANOTHER HOUR of adjustments and testing and warnings about not overdoing it, watching for hot spots, and avoiding stump blisters at all cost before I walk out of there.

But I do *walk out of there*.

Hank has given me a cane, so I use it for stability, and although I'm not entirely confident, or even very competent, I *want* to walk and Hank tells me that's ninety percent of the battle won.

On the way home Mom has the brilliant idea that what I need are some of those warm-up pants with zippers that run all the way up the sides of the legs. So we drive downtown to the Sports Stop, and since I'm still in my shorts, I have her go in without me.

She returns with two pairs: one's royal blue and gold— Liberty colors—the other is black with white trim. "These are perfect!" I tell her, and she seems happy.

Really happy.

Dad's happy to see me moving on both legs, too, but he's also fascinated by the leg itself. He wants to hear all about the fitting and the adjustments and how the suction sleeve works, and when he's up to speed on the mechanics of it, he makes me walk across the kitchen about six times.

I think for the first time in ages *he* sees hope.

Kaylee's like, "Wow, you are going to have so much fun on Halloween!" and I give her a friendly punch in the arm for that. And when Fiona hears I'm home and walking, she drops everything and rushes over to the house.

"I'll get it!" I call when the doorbell rings. I've switched into my new warm-up pants, so when Fiona takes me in, all she sees is me in my Nikes.

Exactly how I used to look.

I step back and say, "Come on in."

I try hard to make my gait even as we walk down the hallway. Hank said it's the one thing that gives you away, but that by paying close attention and watching yourself in the mirror, you can master an even gait.

There are no mirrors, so I can't see how I'm doing, but Fiona has a definite opinion. "That's *amazing*," she says, following me into the kitchen.

"She's showing off," my mom scolds. "She's supposed to be carrying a cane."

"Wow!" Fiona says, watching me. "Wow, wow, wow!"

Then I sit down and unzip my pant leg, and her face falls. "It's just a pipe? Aren't they going to, you know, make it look like a leg?"

I shrug. "This one's temporary, and I have to go in every week for adjustments, so it's just a lot more practical to have it like this."

"So when do you get your permanent leg?"

"It depends. Hank thinks I'll be ready in two or three months. They want to make sure my leg is all done changing." I zip down my pant leg and smile at her. "In the meantime, it's good to be walking around."

"Hey!" she says, getting all excited. "You have *got* to show up at the car wash tomorrow, walking! Kyro will be floored! And the car wash is going to be great. Kyro had this huge blue-and-gold banner made. It says HELP JESSICA RUN! And the car wash committee voted to wear track uniforms, so we'll be color-coordinated with the sign!"

I laugh. "You want to be color-coordinated with a sign?"

She scowls at me. "It'll make us more visible and show that we're a team, working toward something."

"Wait. I thought you were on the bake sale committee."

She grins. "Come on. I'm on all the committees!"

I laugh. "Figures."

"So you'll come?"

How could I not?

I hug her and tell her I'll be there.

chapter 18

IT'S AMAZING HOW TWO THIN PIECES of clothing can hold such deep memories. Laughter, pain, victory, defeat, friendship, fatigue, elation . . . they're all there, but only to the person who's worn the uniform. To the rest of the world it's simply shorts and a tank top.

Fiona told me to wear them to the car wash, but holding the gold shorts and Liberty singlet now makes me feel like an impostor.

Still, I finally take a deep breath and pull them on.

The fabric is cool and smooth against my skin.

Memories tingle through me.

I sit on the edge of my bed for a long time, fighting back tears. Why am I wearing a track uniform? What am I *thinking*? Each of yesterday's steps was careful, calculated, conscious. I can't see them ever being anything but.

And that's just *walking*.

Then I remember Chloe.

And the YouTube athletes.

They make movement, *running*, look so natural.

So easy.

How do they *do* that?

I finally put on my leg and pull on my new blue-and-gold side-zip sweats. I feel better covered up. Like less of an impostor.

Going downstairs, I navigate the steps carefully. I feel clunky and clumsy and slow, and I'm glad for the handrail. I actually think about sitting and scooting, but I do make it down without cheating.

I find my parents in the kitchen. "So who wants to drive me to the car wash?" I ask, putting on a brave face. "Or can I just drive myself?"

I'm joking, but Dad takes me seriously. "I'll drive you," he says quickly, and before long we're on our way to the gas station on the corner of Grand and Highland.

The first thing I see is the banner.

HELP JESSICA RUN!

The colors are bright and it's way bigger than I'd imagined. And it's strange to see my name up there.

Like it must be another Jessica, not me.

There are blue and yellow balloons punching around in the wind, and two bake sale tables set up with blue and yellow tablecloths, and about twenty-five or thirty people in blue-and-gold track uniforms. Some of the runners are washing cars, some are working the bake sale tables, and some are holding poster-board signs and shouting at cars from the corner.

"Wow," my dad says when he sees the setup.

"How lucky am I, huh?"

He gives me a curious look but then nods as he turns into the parking lot. "Luckier than I knew."

He pulls to a stop and asks, "Is this good?"

"Great!"

"You need help?"

I open the van door and carefully step down. "Nope!" I say from the ground. Then I grab my cane, blow him a kiss, and close the door.

chapter 19

I GET MOBBED BY MY TEAMMATES, and of course they all want to see the leg.

Until they do.

The girls try not to show it, but they are horrified.

"Oh my God, it's just a *pipe*."

"Aren't they going to make it look, you know, *real?*"

The guys, though, think it's wicked cool.

"That is *tight*, man!"

"Yaz! Dude! Come here! Check out Jessica's leg!"

"Wow, that is *crazy*. . . . That's, like, Terminator tough!"

I tell myself that the guys being wowed and the girls being revolted is better than the other way around, but both extremes are a little much.

Kyro intervenes. "Hey, people. Get back to your posts! We're trying to make some money here!" Everyone but Fiona scatters, and he smiles at me and says, "It's great to see you out here. And it's great to see you in uniform."

"Her idea," I say, hitching a thumb at Fiona.

"Well, it's a good one."

I zip down my pant leg and say, "It's not pretty, I know, but it's nice to be able to walk again."

"I'll bet it is," he says with a laugh. "And it *is* the first step to running again." He looks around. "Good turnout, huh?"

I nod.

Even Merryl is there, working the bake sale table.

But after a while it becomes clear that the turnout is really mostly people from the track team and their parents.

I help out at the different tables and talk to people, but after being there almost an hour, I'm getting the picture that there's not enough work to go around. Then I hear "Hey, Jessica!" from across the lot.

"Yeah?" I call back.

"Get over here!"

It's Graham DeBlau and Mario Reed. Graham's a vaulter, Mario's a sprinter. Right now they're both wavers, flagging me out to the sidewalk.

So Fiona and I make our way over to them.

"You're wearing shorts, right?" Graham asks.

I nod.

"So take off those sweats and stand here with us."

Mario adds, "A *lot* more people will stop."

I blink at them. "No way! I'd be like . . . a *freak* show!"

"Look," Graham says. "How are people supposed to understand what we're doing? How are they supposed to know who Jessica is?"

"Yeah," Mario chimes in. "Maybe the bus wreck was in the news, but people forget."

I look at Fiona for help, but she just shrugs and says,

"I totally get why you wouldn't want to, but it would explain more than any sign, that's for sure."

Two other runners have been listening in—Colin Johnson and Melanie Matta. Colin says, "You should also hold a sign that says I'M JESSICA."

"No!" I snap.

"How about one that says HELP ME RUN," Melanie suggests.

I cringe. "I would feel like a beggar."

"Look," Graham says. "You need to help us out here."

What they're saying is true.

I know it is.

But standing on the street with my pipe leg and a sign?

It would be so embarrassing.

So . . . icky.

Still. They're all doing this for me. Shouldn't I be helping out the best way I can?

"How about a sign that says I WANT TO RUN AGAIN," Fiona asks quietly. "That's not begging. That's just stating a simple fact."

I look around at their expectant faces.

I do want to run again.

I do want to help.

I take a deep breath. "Okay. Somebody make me a sign!"

chapter 20

HAVING ME OUT ON THE SIDEWALK WORKS.

It also almost causes a couple of fender benders. I guess carrying a sign gives people license to stare, double-take, and rubberneck.

There are no actual accidents, though, just a steady stream of customers. A lot of them aren't so much interested in getting their car washed as they are in writing a check. I see them talking to Kyro. I see them glancing at me. I see them shaking their heads and pulling out their wallets. Some of them even come up to me and tell me stories about their uncle, or their dad, or their army buddy who served in Iraq. They treat me like they've known me my whole life. I guess they're trying to make me feel better.

Or not alone?

But it's kind of bizarre to have people I don't even know telling me these personal stories. Especially the gruesome ones about Iraq. I'm not up for hearing all those details, but what am I supposed to do?

I just smile and nod and take it.

Then Gavin Vance arrives.

I'm suddenly and completely re-embarrassed.

I want to pull on my sweats.

Hide.

I try to get back to simply holding my sign, but I can't help sneaking looks at him.

He hugs Merryl, who is ecstatic to see him.

They laugh.

Hold hands.

She feeds him a brownie.

I force myself to stop looking, but I can't seem to quit wondering if any guy—Gavin or otherwise—will ever look at me.

Will ever want me.

It's not the first time I've thought this, but seeing Gavin and Merryl together makes the thought feel so . . . raw.

I glance over my shoulder again and see that Gavin's now talking to Kyro.

A minute later he's still talking to Kyro.

Fiona's been observing all this too, and when Gavin starts to leave, she mutters, "He couldn't even come over and say hi?"

But Gavin doesn't go back to his car. He dashes across the street while traffic is held back by the red light.

"What is he doing?" Fiona asks.

"Running?" I say with a twinge of sarcasm.

When he gets to the center divider, he turns and faces us, then produces a camera and motions for us to hold our signs higher.

"Oh," Fiona says. "Newspaper."

I'm *really* upset now. "I don't want to be seen like this in the school newspaper!"

"It'll get donations," Fiona says, and nudges my arm up. "Just hold up your sign."

Before I can even think to yell, Hey! You need my permission to do that! Gavin has already taken some shots and is running back across the street. And in a flash he's inside his car and driving away.

I don't say anything, but I'm kind of mad at Fiona.

And I'm *really* mad at Gavin.

He should have at least asked!

So I decide—Monday morning, I'm going to find him and put a stop to him using those pictures.

chapter 21

THE CAR WASH EVENT brings in a whopping $876.50. I'm amazed, Kyro's pleased, the team's excited, and Dad is *very* impressed. "Eight hundred and seventy-six dollars?" he asks on the way home.

"And fifty cents," I add. "Someone baked that extra brownie, you know. It counts."

He smiles and nods. "Let's not forget the fifty cents."

But after I'm home for a little while, I start feeling deflated. And *sore*. I can't walk evenly, my body is tender all over, my stump is throbbing. . . . I need to take my leg off and rest. By bedtime I realize that I way overdid it.

I fall asleep easily, but I don't sleep well. It hurts to roll over. I'm too hot, then too cold. And then I have the running dream again.

Only this time I'm not really running.

I'm clomping.

Sherlock is barking at me to hurry up. He runs ahead, turns, barks; runs ahead, turns, barks. I know what he's saying: *C'mon, let's go. Let's GO.*

But I can't. No matter how hard I try, all I can do is clomp along.

Clomp, clomp, clomp.

I look down and see my leg.

It's just a big steel pipe.

No foot, no shoe.

Clomp, clomp, clomp.

Bark, bark, bark!

Clomp, clomp, clomp.

Bark, bark, bark!

Clomp, clomp—I wake up with a jolt to find my mother on the edge of my bed. She's holding the phone and the Sunday paper, which is still in its dew-proof bag. "Sorry to wake you," she whispers.

"That's okay," I murmur, glad to be out of the dream.

She hands over the phone. "It's Fiona. She says it's important, and that I should give you this." She puts the newspaper next to me.

"Hello?" I say into the phone.

"Have you opened the paper?" she asks.

"No," I mumble. "I'm still asleep." I eye the clock. It's not even seven.

"Well, wake up! You are on the front page of the Community section!"

"I am?" I ask, still groggy. "How?"

"Gavin wrote an article. It's amazing!"

Now I'm awake. "Gavin did?"

"Yes! And there's a huge picture of *you*. Open . . . the . . . paper!"

Mom's giving me a questioning look, so I tell her, "Can you open the paper? Go to the Community section."

"Section C," Fiona says in my ear.

But Mom finds the section without any extra help. She pulls it out, unfolds it, and we both gasp.

There's an enormous picture of me—just me—holding up my sign.

I WANT TO RUN AGAIN

So much for my stopping him from using the picture.

But strangely, I'm not mad.

I'm more in shock.

Fiona can tell we've found the article. "Call me back when you've read it," she says with a laugh, then hangs up.

The headline is "Getting Back on Track."

The byline is "Gavin R. Vance."

Mom's hands are shaking, so I snatch the paper from her and hold it steady so we both can read.

> Jessica Carlisle was a world-class runner. Or, according to her track coach, Leonard "Kyro" Kyrokowski, well on her way to becoming one. "She set a new league record in the 400-meter race just hours before the accident. She had the discipline, the determination. She had incredible potential."
>
> The accident to which Kyrokowski refers involved a school bus transporting the

> Liberty High School track teams and an
> uninsured junkyard hauler named Jack
> Lowe. . . .

"Even if I didn't know you," my mom whispers, "I'd read this article. It pulls you right in!"

"Shhh," I tell her, and together we continue to read all about the accident and the track team's quest to buy me a running leg. There's a nice, smaller picture of the track team working the car wash, and a sidebar that has the heading "Help Jessica Run Again" and gives the school's contact information for anyone who wants to donate money. The whole page is put together very well, but it's the closing part of the article that really gets me.

> Jessica Carlisle may have lost a leg, but
> she has not lost her spirit. Last Thursday
> she was back at the track, cheering from
> the sidelines as her teammates battled
> Langston High in a dual league meet.
> Next year she'd like to be back *on* the
> track.
> Running.

"This is a wonderful piece," my mother sniffs, brushing away a tear. She points to the byline. "Do you know the writer?"

I hesitate.

Do I *know* him?

He gives amazing speeches, writes fantastic op-eds and now newspaper features, spearheads community warmth drives . . . and he dates a manipulative ditz.

My mother prompts, "You said, 'Gavin did?' to Fiona."

I concede with a little nod. "He's in our class, but I don't really *know* him."

"Well," she says, easing the paper away from me, "I'm sure Kyro has his number. You should call him. This definitely deserves a thank-you."

She leaves—no doubt to show Dad the article. And I know I should be calling Fiona back, but I just sit there for the longest time trying to sort through the collision of feelings I have about Gavin Vance.

chapter 22

I DO TRY TO REACH GAVIN, but the message machine seems to be the only one home. I hang up the first couple of times, but on my third try I leave a message. It's a pretty lame one. Incoherent, really. And right before I hang up, I rattle off my phone number, then immediately wish I hadn't.

What's he supposed to call back for?

To tell me to learn to leave a message?

I don't even *want* him to call back. I already said thank you—what's left to say?

Still, every time the phone rings, I jump a little. Every time it turns out to be someone else on the line, I scold myself.

But Monday morning when he sees me from across the courtyard and leaves Merryl's side to come talk to me, I feel my cheeks flush. I try to be cool and blithely witty as we talk, but me making him laugh makes me laugh, and when he finally goes back to Merryl, I realize that my eyes are shining and my cheeks ache from smiling so much.

Suddenly I feel like crying.

What an idiot I am!

I escape the courtyard, and for the rest of the week I avoid him. I stay away from the main hangouts, I hide out in Kyro's classroom or drag Fiona into Room 402 at lunch, and I focus on important things like schoolwork and walking.

Especially walking.

I work really hard on my gait.

On my roll-off.

On mastering ramps.

By Thursday I'm confident enough to leave my cane at home, which feels like a huge step forward, and random people who I don't even know tell me how awesome it is to see me walking.

But then comes a huge step back.

At lunch Kyro breaks it to Fiona and me that Gavin's newspaper article has brought in only forty dollars. "I don't understand it," he says, raking his long fingers along his hair. "I was sure there would be an outpouring of goodwill."

"Maybe it's still coming?" Fiona says.

He sighs. "Let's hope. Unfortunately there's often a deep, wide abyss between good intentions and concrete action. And as unfair as it is, after a few days any story becomes old news." He looks at me. "It's disappointing, but don't worry. We'll raise the money."

Still. I can't help but be discouraged, and Rosa picks up on my mood in math.

What's wrong? she writes in a note.

The running leg's a pipe dream.

She slips the note back.

So was walking.

Ms. Rucker is watching me, so I hide the note and focus on the board.

Until Rosa slides another note my way.

Don't look so far ahead.

I slip the note into my backpack and find my mood spiraling even further downward. Looking ahead is what's been giving me hope. I've wanted to believe that somehow we'll be able to gather twenty thousand dollars. I've wanted to believe that I'll run again.

But hope now feels so fragile.

Too fragile to touch.

chapter 23

AFTER SCHOOL I SEE THE TRACK TEAMS loading onto a bus.

I stand in the distance and watch, feeling cold and shaky.

How can they even get on a bus?

I remind myself that it's not their first away meet since the wreck. There have been two of them, plus the Glenwood Relays.

For them the memory must be fading.

For me it feels like yesterday.

And every tomorrow, for as far as I can see.

chapter 24

FRIDAY WHEN I VISIT HANK, he's very impressed.

"Fantastic," he says over and over. "Now *that's* progress."

My mom and I exchange glances, and I can tell she's thinking what I'm thinking: Hank seems so different. It's like he's come to life because the monster he's built has come to life.

He makes lots of little adjustments with his Allen wrench, twisting it inside the little holes in the pipe couplings as he throws around words like *adduction* and *abduction, dorsiflexion* and *plantar flexion, inversion* and *eversion.* He makes me walk, he adjusts, he makes me walk, he adjusts . . . and when he's finally done, he smiles at me. "I saw the article in the paper. Great piece. And if your progress this week is any indication, I have no doubt that you will be running again. Soon."

"Thanks," I tell him, and it is nice to see him so enthused. The problem, though, is that his enthusiasm doesn't stick on me. It's been a long, hard week, and all I can seem to see is that I'm still having trouble walking.

PART IV

Adjusting the Blocks

chapter 1

IT'S STILL DARK OUTSIDE. The streetlights glow through the curtains, putting a soft spotlight on Sherlock, who is fast asleep on my bed. He's curled up next to Lucas the bear near the footboard, his back resting against the wall, his chin on the bedspread facing me. Even in his sleep, he's watching me.

Protecting me.

I admire his beautiful coat, the dark lines of his eyes, his pointy ears and droopy whiskers.

I want to kiss his muzzle and tell him what a sweet, sweet boy he is.

And then I get the feeling.

The one I've kept buried for so long.

I have to get up.

Get out.

Go.

Maybe I can do it, I tell myself. Not fast, not hard . . . but maybe I *can* run.

"Sherlock." It's barely even a whisper, but his eyes fly open. "You want to go for a—" I stop myself. "Outside?"

He cocks his head, not entirely sure whether what he thinks I'm asking is what I'm really asking.

For that matter, neither am I.

"Get your Frisbee," I tell him.

He jumps off the bed and darts down the stairs, but he knows it'll be a little while before I can get down there.

I slip on the nylon, then pull on a stump sock.

I layer on another sock.

My leg's still shrinking, so I need the extra padding to keep my socket snug.

Then I put on the liner, push into my pipe leg, and roll up the suction sleeve.

It feels solid, but still . . . foreign.

Like we're still getting to know each other.

I sit on the edge of the bed and dress, pulling on my zip sweats, lacing on my left shoe, zipping up a sweatshirt.

I'm better at the stairs now but still very careful.

Up is easier than down.

Sherlock waits patiently at the bottom, tail wagging, Frisbee at his feet. "Good boy," I whisper, then leave a quick note and ease out the front door.

The air is cool and moist from a light fog—perfect running weather. I breathe in deeply and close my eyes. Something in my mind doesn't know I can't run. Something inside me believes I can just take off.

Sherlock puts down the Frisbee and looks up at me. He's holding his breath. Hoping.

I pick up the Frisbee and say, "Heel."

He falls into place on my left side as we go down our

walkway, but he's keyed up, waiting for something big to happen.

When I get to the sidewalk, I turn left instead of our usual right.

I sense his confusion.

His disappointment.

"Fetch!" I tell him, and toss the Frisbee a straight, controlled distance down the sidewalk.

He tears off after it, and while he's gone, I take a few jogging steps.

It's enough to tell me that I cannot run.

Sherlock is already back.

I toss the Frisbee again.

I try jogging again.

I make it ten steps this time.

Twenty the next.

But it doesn't feel right. It doesn't feel like running. It doesn't feel like anything but hard, hard work.

I think of Kaylee, counting steps.

I try again; try not to count.

I feel like a lifeless machine moving forward.

I rest at the corner, more disappointed than tired. Sherlock, however, is enjoying the Frisbee game immensely, and so we turn the corner and press on. I try jogging a few more times, but eventually I just give up and walk. I tell myself I should be happy with walking.

Walking is a miracle.

I press on, and then through the misty air I hear my name.

It's soft, drifting toward me from the left.

"Jessica!"

I turn, and it's like I'm thrown into a dream. There's a mermaid fountain in the middle of the yard and, beyond it, a girl sitting on the porch, wrapped in a white blanket.

"Rosa?" I ask.

"Jessica!" she says again.

It takes me a moment to understand that I'm *not* dreaming. When I do, I clap twice, bringing Sherlock running back to me, and we both head up the walkway. There's a ramp up the side of the porch steps, just like there still is on ours. "I can't believe you're up so early," I say with a laugh.

"Look who's talking," she says back.

"But . . . why are you out here?"

"I love mornings," she says. "They're so peaceful." She's got her eye on Sherlock. "He's gorgeous!"

"Sherlock, this is Rosa," I say, making the official introduction. "Say hi."

"*Aaarooo!*" Sherlock says, wagging his tail.

Rosa reaches out tentatively to pet him.

"He's very friendly," I say, sitting on a bench that's near her wheelchair. "Don't worry." Soon she's hugging Sherlock around his neck, giggling from being slobbered with doggie kisses.

"You were taking him for a walk?" she asks when Sherlock's settled down a little.

I shrug. "I actually wanted to see if I could run." I eye her and add, "Which I can't."

"You will, though," she says with her lopsided smile. "I put that article on my bedroom wall."

"You did?"

She nods. "It's so cool." Then she says, "Tell me about running. Why do you like it?"

No one has ever asked me this so directly before. Either people like running or they don't. Either people get it or they don't. And if they don't, they just think people who like it are crazy.

Which is okay.

That makes us even.

But now I have to explain *why* I like it, and I'm not sure where to start. "Uh . . . running, or racing?"

She thinks, then says, "Running. Like this morning."

"Hm." I try to put my finger on it. "Because it feels like freedom?"

She nods thoughtfully.

"And your mind travels places where it doesn't normally go. . . ."

"Huh?"

"Like dreaming in real time?" I laugh. "Never mind. It sounds crazy."

She laughs too, so I say the next thing that pops into my mind. "I love the morning air on my face—it's one of the best things about running. The rest of your body's warm, but your face is cool." I laugh again. "I totally get why dogs like to stick their head out of car windows. Running's like that but with fewer bugs in your teeth."

She laughs again, then sighs and says, "I wish I could feel that."

"What?" I kid her. "Your mom won't let you stick your

head out the window while she's driving? What kind of mom do you have?"

"A good one!" Then she says, "Now racing."

"Huh? Oh—what do I like about racing?"

She nods, so I give *that* some thought and finally tell her, "It's electric. From stepping into your lane until you cross the finish line . . . every cell of your body is charged."

"Going over the finish line must be wonderful."

I laugh. "Especially if you're the first one there."

"But . . . it means you finished. You made it. Even if you don't get a medal."

I look at her. "You're very philosophical about the finish line."

She gives a thoughtful nod. "It's symbolic." I nod too, because I'm sure I know what she means, but then she adds, "Because it's also the starting line."

For some reason this thought startles me. And I think about all the races where this is true—the 400, the 800, the 1600, all the relays—and it shocks me that I have never looked at it this way.

Maybe because of staggered starts.

Maybe because starting *feels* so different from finishing. At the starting line you're amped, set, coiled. At the finish line you're completely spent.

So the thought that they're the same line gives me a very strange feeling.

A sort of *uncomfortable* feeling.

Like discovering someone very close to you has been leading a secret double life.

chapter 2

MONDAY DURING MATH Rosa slips me a note:

Running or racing, which would you choose?

She slips me questions like this a lot.

Or statements.

Or combinations.

Baby steps are blessings.

Wind is mysterious. Where does it go?

Sometimes they seem so off-the-wall, but they always make me think. This time I consider the question, but I also think about Rosa thinking about running. Why does she spend her time pondering something she'll never be able to do? Why is she interested in it at all? Why in the world would she philosophize about the finish line?

I jot back, *Running.*

I know immediately that it's what I'd choose.

Still.

It's the first time I've actually thought about it.

chapter 3

By Tuesday we've given up on getting more donations from Gavin's newspaper article.

It's been over a week, and they just haven't arrived.

Wednesday morning the bake sale table is missing from the courtyard, and at lunch there's only one person staffing it. Plus all the "baked goods" are store-bought, so no one's buying.

Then Thursday morning there's a message in the announcements: *All track team members are to report to Coach Kyro's classroom at lunch. Be prompt. No exceptions.*

"Sounds ominous," Fiona mutters.

"Maybe it's just about today's meet?"

She shakes her head. "We went over that at practice yesterday."

By lunch I've convinced myself that the meeting is to scold the team for giving up on raising money for my leg, and I walk into Kyro's room feeling dread.

Why should my team be expected to raise twenty thousand dollars?

It's crazy.

What's worse is I don't want them to resent me. Or feel like failures because they couldn't do the impossible.

Within the first five minutes of lunch, over ninety people have crammed into Kyro's room. Even Merryl.

"Guys!" Kyro finally says, holding one graceful hand high. "I'll make this quick."

Everyone falls silent.

"Item one!" he says. "I've noticed a lackluster attitude growing among you."

I close my eyes and think, *Oh boy. Here we go.*

He levels a look across the room. "That didn't take long. We've been fund-raising for two weeks, and already you give up?"

No one moves a muscle, but I can feel it—everyone's shrinking away from me.

"Where's your spirit?" he asks. "Where's your determination, your drive? You hit a little headwind and let it knock you flat? Hasn't being on this team taught you that around the bend of every headwind comes a tailwind?"

We just look at him.

"Item two!" he says. "The office delivered this to me today." He holds up a stack of envelopes. "For some reason the helpers in the front office didn't know who to give 'Jessica' mail to, so they collected it in a box." He smiles at us. "So here's our tailwind. The checks range from five dollars to two hundred and fifty, and our new grand total is four thousand seven hundred and sixty-five!"

A roar fills the room.

"Item three!" he shouts, and we all fall quiet. "We have a patron. Someone who insists on staying anonymous. They have pledged a dollar for every dollar we raise, up to ten thousand dollars."

"Wait," Mario Reed says. "So that means we're already up to . . . like . . . ninety-five hundred?"

"Very good!" Kyro says. He looks around the room. "We are almost halfway there, people!"

Cheers fill the room again, and this time people pump fists and pat me on the back and give me double thumbs-up.

Kyro lets it go on for a minute before raising his hand again. "Last item!"

"There's more?" people whisper to each other.

"We will have visitors at our meet this afternoon. Channel Seven is sending a local news crew out to do a story on the team, and on Jessica."

"Wait," Mario says again. "We're gonna be on TV?"

Kyro nods. "They saw the article in the paper and want to help get the word out." He looks at me. "You will be there today, right?"

I'm smiling and laughing and crying all at the same time.

"You bet," I tell him as I wipe my face dry.

"How do you feel about wearing a uniform?"

I hesitate. It was one thing to wear it at a car wash when I didn't know I was going to be in the paper. It's another to wear it knowing I'll be on TV.

Mario starts a chant. "Do it! Do it! Do it!"

It doesn't take long for everyone to chime in. "Do it! Do it! Do it!"

I pinch my eyes closed.

How can I not?

"Okay," I blurt out. "I'll do it!"

"YAY!" the team cheers.

"Remember, people," Kyro calls out. "This is the last league meet. Let's win this thing!"

From the roar that follows, there's no doubt that that's exactly what they plan to do.

chapter 4

THE TEAM IS LOVING having a news crew around. They make a show of everything, especially crossing the finish line. So far the crew is not talking to me, so I try to forget they're even there and not feel too self-conscious about my very visible fake leg. I do my best to act normal, and I shadow Fiona as she moves from event to event.

The only time I really forget about my leg is when Shandall comes in second in the 100-meter dash. I cheer my head off for that, because she usually gets edged back to fourth, and the best she's placed all year is third.

"Way to *go*, Shandall!" I yell as she prances into the infield.

She works her way over to me. "That felt so good," she pants. "Girl, I was *flyin'*."

"Yes, you were!" I bump her fist when she puts it up. "Flying with *flames* shooting from your feet!"

Shandall laughs. "Glad you could see 'em, 'cause I could sure feel 'em!" She cocks her head at something behind me and lowers her voice. "You've got company."

I turn around and see the TV news crew standing behind me. "Jessica?" the news lady asks. Her blond hair is tied down with a scarf. She's wearing a designer sweat suit and cute little Pumas—nothing like what she wears when she's anchoring the news. "I'm Marla Sumner. It's a pleasure to meet you."

I shake her hand. She's smaller than she looks on TV. And even prettier.

"This is my photographer, Andy Richards," she says, indicating the man lugging a large black camera bag, a tripod, and a big-lens video camera.

He flashes a smile, then gets busy with his equipment.

"Your coach says you're okay with being interviewed?"

I nod.

"Good." She looks around, then points to a spot farther infield. "Why don't we do it over there. I'd like to get the finish line in the background."

It doesn't take long for them to set up. Marla tells me to look at her, not the camera, and the first thing she has me do is state my name. After that she's off and running with questions. I'm nervous at first, but since the camera's a little off to the side, I try to block it out and just answer her questions. She's very attentive and nods a lot, and before too long she's done. "Thank you so much, Jessica," she says. "This is an important story, and we want to do what we can to help."

"I appreciate that," I say softly.

"How do you feel about us coming to your home? I think it would add a personal dimension if we could include your family in the story."

"Uh, I think that would be okay. You should ask my mom and dad, though."

So I give her our phone number, thank her again, and set out to find Fiona, because her heat of the 800-meter has just been called.

I run into Gavin Vance instead.

"Hey!" he says. "I heard the good news!"

I look down, because holding his gaze is just . . . unnerving. "Nice little snowball you got rolling." I glance up. "Thanks."

"Hey, if it wasn't a worthy story, they wouldn't be here."

"Thanks," I tell him again, then start moving across the infield.

"It's Fiona's race, right?" he asks, following me. "You heading up to Rigor Mortis Bend?"

I cock my head a little. "Wow. You better watch out. People might start thinking you're part of the team."

This seems to please him, and he falls into step beside me as I trek up to the 300-meter mark. "I'm starting to feel a little like it, actually."

I snort. "Yeah? Well, you've got a lot of wind sprints to catch up on, buddy."

He laughs, then says, "But I did take your advice."

"About?"

"Running for more than just office."

I keep moving. "So you what? Went for a run?"

He nods. "I've been a few times, actually." He laughs again. "The first one was torture. It's been a long time." We walk in silence for a few steps, and then he says, "You're amazing!"

This catches me off guard, until I realize he's talking about the fact that I'm walking on a pipe.

"Kyro asked me to wear the uniform," I say with a frown. "I'm not trying to be an exhibitionist or anything."

"Are you kidding me? Who thinks that?" He shakes his head. "Do you realize how fast you're walking?"

The gun's gone off for Fiona's race, so I pick up the pace even more.

"There's no stopping you, is there?" he says with a chuckle.

"Not where Fiona's concerned," I tell him. "She has been the most incredible friend."

I don't know if it's my comment about Fiona or him not wanting to leave me alone on Rigor Mortis Bend, but he stays there with me. I cheer for Fiona on her first lap, and when she hits the 600-meter mark on her second time around, she's trailing the first-place runner from Hartwell, but not by much.

When she crests the curve and hits the bend, I can see the grit on Fiona's face. The focus. I shout, "You can do it, Fiona—pass her!"

Gavin cheers her on too, and it's cute because you can tell he's never actually done this before. Words come out, but they're shy. He's shouting, but there's nothing really *loud* about it.

When Fiona hits the straightaway, her head bobs and she bears down, moving out a lane to pass the girl from Hartwell.

"Kick it, Fiona! Kick it in!" I shout, and then hold my breath as she edges ahead and wins the race.

"She did it! She did it!" I squeal. And I find myself

jumping and hugging—just like I would with anyone else on the team.

Only this isn't just anyone.

This is Gavin Vance.

And it's my first physical contact with him of any kind. I've never even accidentally bumped or brushed or *touched* him before.

And now I'm hugging him?

"Sorry!" I say, pulling away. Then I try to cover up my embarrassment with words. "It's just . . . you have no idea how hard the eight hundred is. There's no way you could get me to run that race. It's the four hundred times two! Rigor Mortis Bend *twice*. I have trouble facing it even once!" I start moving away from him. "Well, I'm going to go congratulate her. Thanks for helping cheer her on."

And I escape.

Not that there's any danger of him following me.

Not with Merryl making a beeline toward him the way she is.

chapter 5

BOTH VARSITY TEAMS WIN HANDILY against Hartwell, and the JV boys and girls squeak by.

But it's still a sweep, and everyone is pumped.

Merryl's nowhere to be found, but what else is new? And since Gavin disappeared with her, it's easy for me to just celebrate the moment with my team.

Afterward Fiona drops me at home, and to my surprise, the Channel 7 news van is parked at the curb. When I get inside the house, I hear my dad saying, "They're still arguing about whose responsibility it is, and meanwhile what are we supposed to do? This was a school event. It happened on a school bus."

I can't believe he's telling them this. And the cameraman is getting it all on video!

"Dad!" I say, throwing down my backpack. "What are you trying to do? Get everyone at school to hate me?"

Marla Sumner signals the cameraman to cut, then turns to me. "This is a really important part of the story, Jessica."

"No! The story is that my team is trying to do something

amazing and positive! We do not have to get into all this negative stuff!"

She considers this a moment, then has some silent exchange with my dad before smiling at me and saying, "Your mother told me about Sherlock. Could we get some footage of you and him in your front yard?"

"Sure," I tell her.

Anything to change the subject.

Anything to get her away from my dad.

After about ten minutes outside, Marla and her cameraman pack up and take off. I hang outside with Sherlock a little longer because I'm still upset with my father, but when I go back inside, I discover that *he's* upset with *me*.

He sits me down at the kitchen table.

Mom is standing off to the side, quiet.

"I'm sorry if you think I'm being negative," he says. "I'm sorry if you didn't want me to talk about the school district's obligation to meet your basic medical needs. But here's the reality: While the insurance companies are dragging their feet, I am working twelve, fourteen, sixteen hours a day to keep us afloat. While they're deciding who is responsible for your hospital bills, your mother and I have taken out a second mortgage on the house. It won't begin to pay for everything, but for now it'll put off collection agencies and ruined credit or bankruptcy. Because their lawyers are playing a game of cat and mouse, we've had to hire our own, and he's told us that these kinds of cases usually take *years* to settle. But if we don't fight for your rights now, you will get a measly settlement that won't include the medical care and prosthetic limbs that you'll need in the years ahead. You're still growing, Jessica, and your body will keep changing. Plus prosthetic legs wear out. I've researched this, and you will need dozens of legs in your lifetime. At twenty thousand dollars a pop, that's not something we're willing to let go or pretend isn't a problem. As your parents, we need to prepare for your future. Anything less would be completely irresponsible. So if you think I was being 'negative' with the news crew, I'm sorry. The fact is I'm just looking out for you."

"How was I supposed to know?" I snap. "Why didn't you tell me any of this before?"

"Maybe we should have," Dad says wearily. "But we thought you were dealing with enough already."

I just sit there feeling awful.

I've known that my parents have worries, but I thought they would go away. I figured that in time everything would work itself out.

But while I've been living day to day, worrying about walking, my parents have been taking the long view, thinking about my future.

Before the accident, "my future" just meant college. College is something I haven't thought about since the accident, but Fiona and I did have plans.

Big plans.

And now, thinking about my future, I'm slapped with the reality that attending our dream college is no longer an option for me.

My parents couldn't afford it then.

I'll never get a running scholarship now.

So Fiona will be going there without me.

That thought, along with everything my dad said and the obvious toll this has taken on my parents, hits me in the gut like an unexpected punch. "I'm sorry," I choke out.

Then I go up to my room and cry my eyes out.

chapter 6

I SEEM TO HAVE long heart-to-hearts with everyone that night.

Mom, Dad, Fiona, Kaylee . . . even Sherlock, although the one with him is pretty one-sided. By bedtime I'm sick to death of trying to sort through everything, and I tell Dad that he can call the news station back if he wants to.

He kisses me on the forehead and tells me for the hundredth time that he wishes he could change things. And then, right before he closes my door, he turns to me and asks, "What was Lucy's last name?"

"Lucy? Sanders," I answer. But as he's leaving, I have a horrible thought. "Wait!"

He looks back into the room.

"You can't have her parents depositioned or dispositioned or whatever you were talking about before. Lucy's dead! They're not going to want to talk to lawyers. It would be mean to ask them to help us!"

He gives me a curious look, and I can see him trying to stay calm. "Jessica," he says quietly, "I want to see if I can help *them*."

Then he closes the door.

chapter 7

LEAGUE PRELIMS TAKE PLACE over the weekend. Kyro invites me along, but I'm still not ready to get on a school bus, let alone stay on one for over a hundred miles each way.

Instead, I help Mom in her flower garden. She's bought pansies and vinca and gazania, verbena, impatiens, and marigolds, and sacks of potting soil. She bustles about, uprooting dead plants and weeds, and mulching new life into the tired dirt.

She's late with her planting this year, and she shouldn't have waited. As the day wears on and the new plants get nestled into earth, her whole being seems to change. She hums.

She blooms.

Sherlock is out in the yard with us, gnawing on a stick. He seems content too, ignoring the fluttering birds and the occasional pedestrian.

I think about the seasons.

About the joys of spring.

About the cold, hard days and long, dark nights of winter.

I wonder if old people ever look back on their lives and see it in terms of seasons.

Years of summer.

Decades of spring.

I wonder what I'll see when I look back later in life. Looking back now, I see sixteen years of springtime, followed by a deep, sudden freeze.

I wonder how long this winter will be for me.

I wonder how long I'll have only glimpses of sunshine.

I wonder if it'll ever be enough to thaw the freeze, or if the ice will just soften for a moment, then harden again.

My mother shakes me from my thoughts. "It's so nice to have you out here with me." She takes off her gloves and holds my face. "My family, and my flowers. That's all I need in this world."

I smile and try to hold on to the warmth of her sunshine.

chapter 8

FIONA QUALIFIES EASILY for the league finals in the 800 and the high jump. I had no doubt that she would, but I heap on the praise anyway. "Congratulations!" I gush on our way to school Monday morning. "I want to hear all about it!"

She's happy to oblige but catches herself after a few minutes. "Is this okay to do?"

"Of course it is!" I say, but the truth is, I'm feeling like I really missed out.

She glances at me. "I'm sorry. I'm being an idiot."

"Hey, it's fine! I really want to know." I try to jumpstart her by asking, "So did Vanessa dominate the four hundred?"

Fiona scowls. "Yes. And the hurdles. You should have seen her struttin' around."

"Yeah, well, what else is new?"

She eyes me. "She didn't break your record, though, so nanny on her."

I laugh, "Nanny on her?"

"Yeah," she says, grinning. "Nanny-nanny-nah on her!"

Then she adds, "Oh! And Merryl didn't even bother to show up. Kyro called her at home when the bus was set to leave and her mother said she was sick."

"Yeah, right. But she wouldn't have qualified for finals anyway."

"So? How can she say she's part of the team when she's always skipping out or not showing up? It's, like, cheating."

During the day, though, I bump into Gavin three times, and Merryl is nowhere to be seen. So I start wondering if maybe I've been too hard on her—maybe she really is sick.

Then at lunch Fiona and I are heading toward the courtyard when we run into Gavin *again*. "Hey there," he says, looking maddeningly handsome.

"Hey," I say back. "How's Merryl feeling? I heard she was sick."

"Yeah," he says. "It really knocked her out." He falls into step beside us. "Are you guys eating lunch in the courtyard?"

"Uh, *no*," I tell him. "Actually"—I look at Fiona—"I want to see how Rosa's doing." I pull a goofy face. "For some reason Ms. Rucker thinks us passing notes in math is a *bad* thing, and I really need to catch up with her." Which is true. I haven't had much of a chance to talk with Rosa since that morning on her porch.

Fiona gives me wiggly-faced signals, but I ignore them.

"You can go ahead," I tell her. "I'll catch up with you later." Then I turn down the walkway to Room 402.

But Fiona follows.

And so does Gavin.

"Go on," I tell them. "You don't have to come with me."

"Who's Rosa?" Gavin asks.

"She's a freshman," I tell him.

"She's got cerebral palsy," Fiona whispers.

"She's my *friend* and a math genius," I tell them both, and give Fiona a scolding look. "She's been great to me through this whole thing." I stop and shoo them with my hands. "Go. I'll catch up with you later."

But they don't go.

They follow me.

The Room 402 gang is surprised to see all of us. "Wow," Mrs. Wahl says, "lots of company!"

Billy and Trent seem a little uncomfortable with the invasion. They turn back to their lunches and avoid looking at us. But Alisha and Penny don't mind—they especially seem to like that Gavin's there.

Fiona and Gavin hang out while Rosa and I joke around. The rest of us have lunches from home, but Gavin doesn't, so I ask him, "Don't you want to go get something to eat?"

"No," he says. "I'm good."

So I slip him half of my sandwich.

And half of my SunChips.

And half of my apple slices.

When lunch is almost over, we say our goodbyes to the Room 402 gang, and on the way down the ramp, Gavin whispers, "Can you really understand her? I could only catch a little of what she said."

I nod. "It was hard at first, but now I'm pretty good at it.

It's like a dialect—it takes some getting used to, but you eventually figure it out."

At the bottom of the ramp he turns right toward the courtyard and we turn left toward the 900 Wing. "Catch ya later!" he calls.

And he seems to be smiling at me.

chapter 9

TUESDAY MORNING IN FIRST PERIOD, Ms. Aloi reads the announcements like she does every morning. Most of us doze through it like we do every morning.

Until she reads, "Attention, juniors and seniors. The prom is right around the corner! This year's theme is Hollywood Nights, and formalwear is required. Tickets will go on sale Friday in the activities office. Fifty-five dollars per person, or one hundred dollars per couple. This event is open to juniors and seniors only!"

Fiona and I look at each other, and I roll my eyes.

Like anyone's going to ask me to the prom?

Like I could dance?

Besides, a prom dress and a pipe leg would feel ridiculous together.

Immediately after the prom announcement, Ms. Aloi reads, "All students! Be sure to watch Channel Seven news tonight—a very special program featuring our fantastic track team and their Help Jessica Run campaign will be broadcast. Tell your friends, tell your family, and tune in at five, six, or eleven!"

Ms. Aloi smiles at me. "I'll be sure to do that!"

A little chill runs through me as I realize that Kyro's almost certainly the one behind the announcement, and that he's probably also e-mailed it to every contact he has in the county.

He has no idea the news crew talked to my dad.

Fiona tells me not to worry, but I can't seem to concentrate on anything else all day. During math Rosa slips me a note that says, *I'll be watching the news!* and for some reason it makes me write back a long, scribbled note about being worried and why I'm worried, and how I don't even want it to air.

She writes back, *The truth is always OK.*

I'm studying her message, thinking about what she's written, when I hear, "H-hm."

I look up and see Ms. Rucker standing beside me with her hand out.

"I'm sorry," I say lamely. I start to put the note away, but she stays there with her hand out. So I plead, "It's personal. . . ."

Her hand stays out.

Finally I turn it over to her and watch as she strolls to the front of the class, her long nose buried in my note.

chapter 10

AT FIVE O'CLOCK Mom's setting the recorder so Dad can watch the broadcast when he gets home. Kaylee is sitting cross-legged on the couch, texting her friends, and I'm sweating bullets.

"Relax," Mom says soothingly as she takes her seat next to me. "It's going to be all right."

"You sound like Rosa," I mutter.

"Who's Rosa?"

The Channel 7 news *Live at Five* graphics and music come on. "I'll tell you later," I whisper, and my heart starts hammering madly in my chest.

The camera zooms in on Marla Sumner and her co-anchor, Keith Franks. "Good evening," Keith says. "Tonight at five: What would you do if your teammate was tragically injured on the way home from a meet?" Footage of our track meet with Hartwell appears on the screen. "We'll show you what a Liberty High School team is doing to help their fellow runner get back on the track."

"That's you!" Kaylee squeals.

It's gone in a flash, but it's hard to mistake me for anyone else when I'm wearing shorts.

"But first," Marla says, and then dives into another story.

And another.

Then there are commercials and another story.

And another.

And the weather.

And more commercials.

And before every commercial break, they run a little teaser segment about the track team.

And me.

"They're not gonna show it until the very end," Kaylee grumbles, texting the whole time.

Then all of a sudden Marla Sumner is looking right into the camera, saying, "Finally at five: the story of the Liberty High School track team and the extraordinary efforts they're making to help one of their teammates run again.

"You may recall our coverage of the tragic bus accident that took the life of one young runner, Lucy Sanders. That accident also took the *limb* of sixteen-year-old Jessica Carlisle."

The TV switches from Marla in the newsroom to me walking across the infield. It's shot from behind, and it's strange to see myself from that angle.

What I notice most is that my gait is still uneven.

"Hours before the accident, Jessica set a league record in the four-hundred-meter race," Marla's voice says over the footage. Then the picture switches to Kyro on the field, talking into the news microphone. "She's incredibly talented," he says. "A tremendously gifted runner. Now that she's back on her feet, we want to get her back on the track."

"A seemingly impossible dream," Marla's voice says, "only if you haven't seen the latest advancements in running prostheses."

Over a graphic of a running leg, she goes on to describe how single- and double-leg amputees are able to compete on "sleek carbon-graphite running blades that absorb impact and store energy much like an Achilles tendon."

"Wow," Mom whispers. "She's done her research!"

"But with this dream," Marla's voice continues, "comes a price tag. With fittings, fabrication, and ongoing adjustments, a leg like this costs around twenty thousand dollars. But that's where all four divisions of the Liberty High School track team come in."

Suddenly my friends are on the screen, waving, angling for face time, hamming it up. "She just wants to run again!" they shout in unison.

Then Marla's voice-over is back. "But how can a track team raise twenty thousand dollars?"

There's a tight shot now of Mario Reed and his friends. "We're doing bake sales and car washes!" they shout. Mario looks right into the camera. "But we could sure use some help!"

The shot switches to Annie and Giszelda, who are introduced as "dynamo hurdlers and the best of friends," and while Annie and Giszelda start verbally tag-teaming, the camera pans over to me cheering on Shandall as she fires down the track. "Look at her," comes Annie's voice.

"She's amazing!"

"Like I would be brave enough to be out here?"

"On that ugly pipe? No way!"

"Like any of this was her fault?"

"Nuh-uh!"

"Kyro says we should always find ways to help others, so that's what we're doing."

"Big-time!"

Marla's voice is back now, talking over muted footage of me being interviewed on the infield. "Jessica also seems to have adopted some wisdom from Coach Kyrokowski about the whole matter."

Suddenly my voice cuts in. "He tells us that life isn't about what happens to you, it's about what you *do* about what happens to you." Then I'm out again, and Marla's voice-over returns. "And although she's trying hard to *do* something about her situation, running again will not be an option if she doesn't get a prosthesis designed specifically for running."

"I tried running on this leg the other day," I'm saying as the camera zeroes in on my pipe leg. "It was awful. Just really clunky."

All of a sudden the outdoor shots are done and they're back in the studio. Keith Franks says, "If you want to help Jessica run again, you can." A graphic with contact information appears on the screen as he continues, "There's a fund set up for her, and it's obviously a good cause. Donation information is also available on our website, where we make it easy for you to make a difference." The contact graphic disappears, and Keith says to Marla, "That is some story."

Marla nods. "And there's so much more to it. Jessica's family is drowning in medical bills because she wasn't insured, and the insurance companies are in gridlock over who should foot the bill. The Carlisles have had to take out a second mortgage on their house, her father's working fourteen hours a day . . . and this is just for her basic needs. It's a nightmare."

"But it sounds like the track team is doing what they can to help."

"It's an amazing group of kids, it really is."

"Well, that's it for us," Keith says into the camera. "We'll see you again next time. Thanks for watching *Live at Five!*"

Mom turns off the recorder and says, "That wasn't so bad, was it?"

Kaylee snorts. "Are you kidding? It was great." She's back to texting, but she takes a second to look at me. "You're a celebrity!"

"Oh, right," I laugh, but seeing everything my team is doing for me condensed into a three-minute broadcast has made me feel good.

Really, really good.

chapter 11

THE NEXT MORNING, Fiona and I run into Annie and Giszelda in the courtyard. "You guys were awesome!" I tell them. "So funny."

"The word," Annie says with a haughty look, "is 'lively.'"

"Yes," Giszelda says, looking down her nose at me. "We are *lively*."

"Indeed," I say with a laugh. "And funny, too."

Shandall joins us, and I say, "Speedy Feet! You were on TV!"

"I looked good, too, didn't I?" she says with a grin, then hugs me. "Girl, I am so happy for you. You are going to have that running leg in no time!"

Then Mario and Graham and Melanie and Colin and a bunch of other track people join us, and our little gathering turns into a full-on celebration.

The whole day is like that. It's really upbeat.

Really *fun*.

Even Ms. Rucker manages to say something nice. Well, for her anyway. "I hope your parents found a good lawyer. The situation's ridiculous." Then she gets back to business, arching one eyebrow as she zeroes in on me. "Next note you pass puts you back in your assigned seat."

I grin at her. "Yes, ma'am."

There's an odd sort of twitch at the corner of her mouth before she turns and walks to the front of the classroom.

Rosa has rolled up in the middle of this, and when Ms. Rucker is far enough away, she whispers, "Was that a smile?"

"That may be as close as she gets," I whisper back.

Rosa pulls her binder out of a saddlebag. "Gavin came into our lunchroom today. He was looking for you."

"What? He did?" I'm embarrassed by how excited I sound.

"Uh-huh." She gives me a lopsided smile. "He's really cute."

I tone things *way* down. "He has a girlfriend, Rosa. A really pretty one."

"Merryl. I know." She eyes me. "He could do a lot better."

The tardy bell rings, and Ms. Rucker wastes no time announcing that there'll be a test on Friday.

I groan, because I am not ready for a test. Not even close. So I really try to focus on the lesson, but I'm having trouble keeping up with Ms. Rucker's overheads.

Rosa slips me a note. *Come over tonight. I'll help you.*

I nod and put the note away, and that night after dinner that's exactly what I do.

"Are you sure you don't want a ride?" my mother asks as I'm heading out the door.

"I'm sure. It's nearby, and Sherlock needs a walk."

"They won't mind him being with you?"

"Rosa loves Sherlock."

She's following me down the walkway. "Tell me again who Rosa is? And how does she know Sherlock?"

"Mom! Stop! It's fine. Everything's fine. Her last name is Brazzi. She's a math genius, and she lives on Marigold Street. I'll call you from her house, okay?"

She lets me go, and as Sherlock and I play Frisbee along the way, I'm really glad I didn't accept a ride. The air's cool, but not cold, and with the days growing longer, there's still plenty of sunlight and lots of spring color everywhere.

Rosa's mother is as happy about me arriving as mine was worried about me leaving. "Jessica!" she says after Rosa has let me in. "I feel like I know you from the paper and the news"—she eyes her daughter—"and of course Rosa has told me all about you." She makes me bring Sherlock in off the porch. "We can't have him miss the party!"

I laugh. "Doing math does not exactly qualify as a party."

But to the two of them it seems to. There's a spread of snacks ready on the kitchen table, with bright blue paper plates and napkins. "This should keep your math energies high," Rosa's mom says.

I do remember to call my mom, and as I'm getting ready to hang up, Rosa's mom says she'd really like to say hello to her. So I turn the phone over, and she takes it into another room to talk while Rosa helps me tackle math at their kitchen table.

Over the next two hours we submerge ourselves in finding

the sums of infinite geometric series, calculating iterate functions, and expanding powers of binomials.

We also manage to eat most of what's on the table.

Finally Sherlock seems to sense that I've had about all the math I can take for one night, because he nudges me from under the table, where he's been curled up, and lets out a little "*Aaarooo.*"

Rosa laughs. "I love the way he talks to you."

Sherlock's head pops up between us, and after Rosa's had a chance to nuzzle with him, I collect my things and say, "All right, boy, let's get going."

"If you come back tomorrow," Rosa says, "I'll give you a pretest."

"What do you mean?"

"Ms. Rucker is very predictable."

"She *is?*"

"I'll make you a test," she says with a nod. "It'll be a lot like hers. You'll see."

If she's willing to do that, I'm willing to try. "Okay," I tell her. "Same time?"

"Same time," she says with a smile.

I thank Rosa and her mom for having me, then head home in the cool night air.

The house is quiet when I get home. It's also dark, except for a little light coming from the kitchen. "Mom?" I call. "I'm home."

"In here," comes her voice from the family room. I find her sitting sideways on the couch, hugging a pillow.

I click on a lamp. "Are you okay?"

"I'm fine," she says with a sigh. Then she tilts her head and asks, "Why didn't you tell me that Rosa has cerebral palsy?"

I sit down beside her and take a deep breath. "I was going to."

"But why didn't you?"

I don't really know where to begin on this. It's been a feeling more than a rational thing, but it's true. I haven't wanted to mention it.

I shake my head. "Rosa and I write notes in class."

She waits. "So?"

"So . . . I didn't talk to her at all before I lost my leg. I ignored her. But now . . ." I lift my backpack and zip open the smallest pouch. "Sometimes she writes things." I pull out my growing collection of her notes. They're little scraps, half sheets, strips. It's a mess, really. It looks like a small pile of garbage.

"You keep them?" she asks.

"I don't really know how to explain it." I sift through the notes. "She has a way of . . ." I look up at Mom. "It's like she opens my eyes."

Mom considers this a moment. "Can you give me an example?"

I'm sifting through the notes again. "Here," I say, pulling one out. "She asked me, *If you could change one thing, what would it be?*" I look up from the note. "Not like a wish; it had to be something real."

"And what did you say?"

"That I could run again. But when I asked her the same

thing, she said"—I turn to the note—"*That people would see me, not my condition.*"

We're both quiet a minute, and then Mom asks, "Do you feel bad because you didn't do that before?"

I almost say yes.

But I stop.

And in that moment I understand why I keep Rosa's notes.

"Not anymore," I say quietly. "I feel good because now I do."

chapter 12

AFTER ROSA'S DONE putting me through my paces the next night, I feel really confident.

"You will get an A tomorrow!" she tells me.

I snort. "That would be a first."

"But not a last!" She's smiling. "You want to come in at lunch for review?"

"I may just do that," I tell her, because I'm making the connection between training to break a league record and training to ace a math test.

Repetition. Effort. Pain. Success.

There really is no shortcut.

So the next day I go to Room 402 at lunch and do my best to volley back right answers to Rosa's ad lib math problems. She baits me to make mistakes by giving problems with my most common weaknesses, but I pull through okay.

When the warning bell rings, she tells me, "You will do great!" but it isn't until math class is over that I believe her.

"How was it?" she asks when the tests are all collected.

"I'm afraid to say . . . easy?"

"Yes!" she says, and surprises me with a fist bump.

We hang around and talk over some of the problems, and then Fiona pops her head inside the classroom. "You ready?" she asks.

"Oh! I forgot!" I turn to Rosa. "Fiona's taking me to Hankenstein's today. It should be my last fine-tuning for a while."

"Have fun," she says, and her face has suddenly gone mischievous.

I turn around and discover that Gavin is now standing in the doorway behind Fiona.

"How would you feel about Gavin coming along?" Fiona asks, her eyebrows going all wiggly.

She's obviously trying to do me a favor.

"Uh . . ."

"It's okay to say no," Gavin says over Fiona's shoulder.

"You can go," Rosa tells him.

I turn to her and whisper, *"What?"* which makes her break out giggling.

"I . . . I don't know," I tell Gavin. But Fiona's giving me a secret fierce look, and I'm feeling a little heady and . . . odd. And they're all staring at me. So I say, "Whatever. If you're sure you want to, fine." Then I turn to Rosa and whisper, "I'm going to sic Sherlock on you this weekend."

She giggles some more.

"See ya, Rosa!" Fiona calls, and Gavin chimes in with "Bye, Rosa," as we leave the classroom.

"Bye, guys!" she calls.

Her voice is happy, but it leaves a little ache in my heart.

She's the one I'd like to take along.

chapter 13

CHLOE IS HAPPY to see that I've got company. And when I make the introductions, she's excited to find out that Gavin is the one who wrote the newspaper article. "It was awesome!" she tells him, then goes on to say how she caught the story on TV. "My friends and I are all rooting for you," she tells me with a big, warm smile.

"Thank you," I answer, but I feel a twinge of selfishness. She's so kind and attentive. It makes it easy to forget that she's had to go through an amputation and rehabilitation too.

Not to mention *cancer*.

I change into shorts, and when I return to the waiting room, Chloe says, "Hank's ready for you. Are you all coming in back, or just Jessica?"

Everyone looks at me.

"Do you *want* to?" I ask.

They say they do, and I guess I feel bad making them stay in the waiting room, so I shrug and say, "Okay."

And it would have been okay, except that after Hank tells me how great the TV news story was, the first thing he does is check my socket fit. He makes me sit down and take off the suspension sleeve, and then he grabs the socket part of my leg and moves it around.

"You're loose. We need to get you into thicker socks."

Off come the leg and the liner.

Off come the socks and the nylon.

Suddenly I'm feeling very self-conscious.

Naked.

Fiona looks down, and Gavin turns away and stays that way.

I'm reminded of how awful it looks. It's not red and swollen—it just looks like flesh—but it's still very graphic.

Very *gone*.

And all of a sudden I'm mortified.

Why in the world did I let them come back here?

Fiona's fine, but *Gavin?*

I'm desperate to get this over with.

To cover up.

To get *out* of here.

Hank has me try on different thicknesses of socks until he's satisfied that my socket fits right. Then we start with the adjustments.

I wish for music.

Conversation.

Sound of any kind.

Finally Gavin breaks the silence, but he looks at Hank, not me. "I saw a man at the airport once who had art painted on his prosthetic leg. It was a sunrise and the ocean. It looked really cool."

"Wow," Fiona says, then asks Hank, "Can you do that?"

"I can do fabric," he says as I begin a test walk for him.

"Fabric?" Fiona asks. "What do you mean?"

"Any piece of cloth. It only takes about half a yard. When I worked in San Francisco, people brought in skull fabric, dolphin fabric, tie-dye, camo fabric . . . you name it. Around here our clients tend to be more conservative." When I turn around, he catches my eye. "We could do that with your definitive leg if you want. It doesn't cost anything extra. I just embed the cloth when I'm making the socket."

Fiona's all excited. "We should go to the fabric store and pick out something really cool! You could do flames or flowers or just a solid, like hot pink!"

I'm holding still now, as Hank's tweaking the adjustments of my top coupling. "But . . . I really just want a leg that looks like a leg. I don't want flames or flowers, and I sure don't want pink."

Hank says, "Well, we can't order your permanent leg until your residual limb is completely stabilized, so you have a couple of months to decide if you want a cosmetic cover or an exposed, artistic socket. Maybe consider it for your running leg?"

Suddenly flames seem like a really cool idea.

I grin at Fiona. "*That* I could get into."

On our way out, Gavin holds doors open for me and makes sure I'm safely in the car before closing my door and getting in back.

"Well," I say as Fiona's driving out of the parking space, "thanks for taking me." I turn to Gavin. "I hope it didn't freak you out too much."

"Not at all," he says.

"So where am I dropping you?" Fiona asks, looking in her rearview mirror.

"Home, if you don't mind," Gavin replies.

"He's just a few blocks past me," I offer. I glance over the headrest. "I used to run by your house to get down to the river."

"I've seen you," he says. "You've got a cool dog."

"Sherlock!" I laugh.

He laughs too. "And your cool dog has a cool name."

Fiona drives to my house, and it's strange—I'm laughing and joking with Gavin like we've been friends forever. And when we get to my house, I'm feeling flushed.

Happy.

I know he has a girlfriend, but he's being really nice to me. Why *did* he want to go to Hankenstein's?

It couldn't just be scientific curiosity.

He gets out of the backseat while I maneuver out of the front, and he holds the door open for me.

"Thanks," I tell him with a smile.

"Sure," he says. "Thanks for letting me tag along."

Then I watch from the sidewalk as he gets into the front passenger seat.

And drives away with my best friend.

chapter 14

IT HITS ME like a ton of bricks.

Gavin wants to spend time with Fiona, not me.

Immediately, I start to make connections.

Who did Gavin help with the WELCOME BACK JESSICA sign in the Greek theater?

Who's bound to have caught his eye while he was with Merryl at the high-jump pit?

Who did he cheer for up at Rigor Mortis Bend?

Who's always there when he comes up to talk to me?

Who is caring and involved and a doer, just like him?

My beautiful, long-legged best friend, Fiona.

Over the weekend my thoughts grow darker.

And darker.

I feel like a total idiot.

What was I *thinking*?

How could I even have hoped that Gavin might actually like me?

How could I have fantasized, even for a minute, that things could be "normal"?

I also can't help but fixate on the fact that while I'm hobbling around at home, Fiona's at league finals *running*.

I was supposed to be there!

I was on track to *win*.

I try to think of good things, but somehow negative thoughts creep in. They take root so easily. Like pesky weeds in a delicate garden.

What I need is a run.

A good, hard run.

To clear my head.

To make me feel whole again.

Instead, I walk Sherlock to Rosa's. She's just back from a CP yoga class—something she says is part of her physical therapy program. I tell her it sounds like a lot more fun than mine.

It's nice to visit with her; nice to laugh a little. But I'm restless and moody, and after about half an hour I leave.

"Cheer up," she calls as I make my way to the sidewalk. "Your finish line is right around the corner."

"Thanks," I call back, and I think about that as I walk home.

Fiona calls late Sunday afternoon, and I make myself sound upbeat. "Hey! How'd it go? Did you place?"

"Nah," she says. "I had kind of an off day. And we got second in league. Langston squeezed us out."

She sounds very low-toned.

Very un-Fiona.

"Oh, I'm sorry," I tell her.

There's a pause and then, "Listen, can I come over?"

"Sure!"

I can tell something's wrong, but it isn't until after she's hung up that I realize what it must be.

I'm right about Gavin.

He's fallen for my best friend.

In the fifteen minutes it takes for her to arrive, I remind myself what an amazing friend she's been. I tell myself I'm happy for the two of them, and I promise myself that I will tell her he's perfect for her, and that I'm so glad my tragedy has brought them together.

I reword that last bit in my mind, then cut it altogether.

When the doorbell rings, I usher her in and hug her and congratulate her on an amazing season and tell her I'm sorry she's bummed.

"I don't know if I'm actually bummed," she says, following me inside.

"So what's wrong, then?"

We settle in on the couch. She takes a deep breath, holds it, then lets it go. "How would you feel if I went to the prom?"

He asked her to the prom?

Not just to the movies?

To the *prom*?

And when did he break up with Merryl?

My heart tries to sink, but I yank it back up.

I can handle this. I'm ready for this. It's okay.

"I'd be really happy for you!" I say with enthusiasm. Then, to save her the trauma of breaking it to me, I ask, "Did he ask after you dropped me off on Friday?"

"Did he . . . ?" She gives me a confused look. "What?"

"Gavin. Did he ask you to the prom after you dropped me off on Friday?"

She looks horrified. "*Gavin?*"

"Fiona, he obviously likes you, and I think you're perfect for each other."

"Shut *up*."

"I do!"

"He doesn't like me! And he has a girlfriend! What are you, crazy?"

There's a lump forming in my throat. I feel so . . . wrecked.

So emotionally wrung out.

She grabs my arm. "*Mario's* the one who asked me to the prom."

"Mario?" I ask, and my chin starts quivering.

"Mario," she says back.

"But I thought . . ." I shake my head. "Why else would he have come along?"

She scoots in and gives me a hug. "You *are* worthy, okay? Quit telling yourself you're not."

All of a sudden I'm crying. "Thanks," I whisper, and hug her tight.

chapter 15

MONDAY BRINGS SOME GOOD NEWS — my first A on a test in Ms. Rucker's class.

"Ninety-three!" Rosa squeals. "Congratulations!" She has her usual one hundred percent, but that doesn't bother me a bit.

I earned a ninety-three!

"Thank you so, *so* much!"

I think Rosa's as happy as I am about my grade. And I guess we're being a bit exuberant, because Eric Hollander in one of the seats in front of us turns around and says, "You got A's? Dude, I got a D."

I snort. "I would have had an F if it wasn't for Rosa." I put my arm around her. "She's an *amazing* tutor."

He scratches his forehead. "I've been going to math lab twice a week, and this is what I get?"

"Forget math lab," I tell him. "Go to Room 402 at lunchtime. Rosa'll whip your grade into shape."

He looks at her. "Really?"

"Any day." She smiles. "I'm good."

I laugh, because "I'm good" is just not something you'd expect from Rosa . . . but it's so true.

He frowns at his paper. "Maybe I'll take you up on that."

I can tell he's in the place I was a month ago—he's thinking that there's got to be some other way to get help. That he'll figure something else out. Something that doesn't require dealing with a girl in a wheelchair.

So after math is over, I hurry to talk to him outside the classroom. "Hey, I know she's hard to understand at first," I say, keeping my voice down. "But that goes away. She's really nice, she's patient, and she's great at explaining math. I'd be flunking without her."

He nods. "Thanks."

I can tell he's still not convinced, so I call after him, "You can always take the course again next year!"

He turns and pulls a horrified face.

I laugh, "Exactly!" Then I call, "Room 402, lunchtime!"

As the week wears on, Gavin bumps in and out of my life. He's nice. Friendly. I do see him with Merryl from time to time, but he also appears out of nowhere a lot. I try hard not to read anything into his presence, but it's an effort.

I try to tell myself that I'm more than a legless girl, but that's an effort too.

Then Thursday during lunch, I decide to stop by Room 402, and to my surprise Eric Hollander is inside getting tutored. I wave a quick hello, then slip out again feeling very . . . I don't know . . . satisfied?

Whatever it is, it feels good.

During math, Rosa jots me a note: *He is so lost.*

I jot back: *You will save him!*

She smiles at me, and later I see her read the note again, then slip it inside her pocket. I think about all the notes from her that I've kept, and I wonder if she knows that she's helped me with much more than math.

It's nice to think I've helped her, too. She *will* save Eric, and when she does, he'll see her, not her condition.

I wish more people could.

chapter 16

FRIDAY MORNING THERE'S A MESSAGE from Kyro in the announcements, commanding all track members to report to his room at lunch to return uniforms and finalize banquet plans. But when Fiona and I arrive, we discover there's a third item on the agenda:

Running-leg money.

After checks started coming in from the newspaper article, Kyro drew a fund-raiser thermometer on his whiteboard, only it's not a thermometer—it's a prosthetic running leg, with zero at the toe and $20,000 at the top of the socket. He's been coloring in the leg with green marker, and anytime anyone wonders how the fund-raising's coming along, all they have to do is look at the board.

Ever since the televised newscast I've been trying *not* to check, but now I can't help but see that the leg is completely colored in.

Actually, it's overflowing.

Kyro asks everyone to settle down, then announces, "This weekend's car wash is hereby canceled, and those of you who are still baking can stop already!" He points to the white-board. "Way to go, people. You did it!"

A loud cheer goes up, and then he continues. "I spoke with our anonymous donor this morning and she—"

"She?" I ask. I know it's hopeless, because I've been nag-ging him about it since he announced that there was an anonymous donor, but I try one more time anyway. "I'd really like to thank her, Kyro. Can't you *please* tell us?"

Kyro realizes he's slipped up, but he shrugs it off with a wave of his hand. "I just eliminated half the population. That's the best I can do. Now, as I was saying, our anonymous donor is still going to send a full ten thousand dollars, even though we've collected nearly fifteen thousand on our own."

"Fifteen thousand?" I look around the room. "You guys are amazing!"

Another cheer goes up, and after Kyro explains that any extra money can go to helping my parents with my medical bills, he calls, "Item two!" and moves on to passing out ban-quet information and checking in uniforms.

While this is going on, I notice Fiona and Mario flutter-ing awkwardly around each other. It's incredibly cute, and pretty obvious that he really likes her. And when people begin filing out of the classroom, Fiona's eyes ask me if it's okay if she leaves with Mario, so I smile and nod, like, Go have fun!

Soon it's just Kyro and me.

"Quite a year," he says to me, and we both laugh at the understatement.

"How can I ever thank you?" I ask quietly.

He smiles at me. It's a kind, tired smile. "Just meet me on the track next year. That'll be thanks enough."

I nod, and even though there's no handshake, the deal is made.

Which means there's no room for excuses.

I'm going to have to learn to run again.

chapter 17

THE REST OF THE SCHOOL YEAR sort of fizzles to an end for me. It feels like a waiting game.

First I wait for the prom to be over. During the weeks leading up to it, everyone seems to pair up. Then the only thing the girls want to talk about is their dresses and how they're going to do their hair, and what their before and after plans are.

Fiona goes to the prom with Mario.

Gavin goes with Merryl.

I stay home and watch TV.

I try to be big about it but can't help wondering if I'd have a date, too, if I wasn't walking around on a pipe. I try to block it out, but the thought keeps springing up.

More weeds in my garden of worthiness.

At the track banquet the team presents me with a check for my running leg, which is an awesome and very emotional thing for me, but when I go to see Dr. Wells, he tells me that my stump is still changing and that I'm not ready for a "definitive prosthesis."

I have to wait until the end of June.

Or maybe July.

The school year closes out with finals and all-too-frequent encounters with Gavin.

I manage to get a B or better in all my classes—even Ms. Rucker's, where I've climbed up to eighty-two percent, thanks to Rosa. It's Gavin I can't seem to figure out. He's still with Merryl, but when I see them together, he looks . . . quiet. When he runs into Fiona and me, he comes to life, laughing and smiling and talking about . . . everything.

But Fiona's still with Mario, and I've still got a pipe leg.

I try not to define myself that way, but I can't help it. And even though my gait is now smoother and people swear they don't even notice, I never forget that under my pants is a pipe.

So the school year fizzles to an end, and I wait.

Fiona keeps me moving forward. She gets us *Preparing for the SAT* books for over the summer, because I didn't take the test this year, and she wants to retake it in November. "This way we'll both be totally prepared. Plus it'll actually be fun to study, 'cause we'll be doing it together and we won't have any other homework!"

I know I'm supposed to take the tests, but it seems so pointless.

You don't need SAT scores to get into the local JC, which is where it looks like I'll be going.

Still. It'll be something to do with Fiona, which is better than doing nothing.

Fiona also manages to get us job interviews at the Tremont Theater. It's an old-timey single-screen movie theater that shows foreign films and cult classics. A funky-cool place that's run by a bohemian grandma named Greta.

I don't mention my leg when I go in to interview, and Greta's got hobbles of her own and doesn't seem to notice that there's anything different about me. She just talks to me about popcorn and pigeons, and hires me on the spot.

Fiona and I don't actually start working there until school lets out for summer, and it turns out to be a pretty fun job. After we're trained, Greta's nice about giving us the same shift, and we do everything from selling tickets and making and selling popcorn to sweeping up between shows and shooing away pigeons.

Kids from school come in—especially the artsy ones. It's kind of nice, because even though it's a totally different crowd from the one I hang out with, they take their movies very seriously.

And then at the end of June Dr. Wells decrees that my leg is stabilized and gives me a prescription for my permanent leg.

Which means I can also get my running leg.

I go through the same routine all over again with Hank—casting, wait a week. Socket fit, wait a week. But then I have to wait another week for the leg fit.

And another week.

Hank has decided that what I need is an active foot for my everyday leg—a "flex foot" that will even allow me to run. "It's not for track work," he tells me, "but it's a very dynamic foot—you'll be amazed."

But there's a part on back order.

A *part* on *back order*.

Somehow I've almost blocked from my mind that I'm an assemblage of nuts and bolts and carbon graphite.

July is almost over when I finally get called in for my fitting. And since, after weeks of proving to her that I can, Mom has finally allowed me to start driving again, she lets me go to Hank's alone. She usually likes to come to my appointments and hover, but she tells me she's swamped. "Would you mind?" she asks.

"Not a bit," I tell her, and it's the truth. I love driving. It did take a little adjusting to learn to drive with my fake leg, because my ankle doesn't flex and I have to control the gas and brake pressure by using my knee and thigh. But I'm good at it now, and it's nice not to have my mom in the passenger seat, scared out of her mind that I'm about to crash.

Plus I know the appointment's going to be a long one.

We've got two legs to fine-tune!

"You've got your cell phone, right?" she asks.

"Right." It's another thing I've had to wait ages for, and now that it's replaced, I don't go anywhere without it.

So I'm feeling, uh, footloose and fancy-free? But when I arrive at Hank's, I learn that the running leg is not done. "A manufacturer delay," Chloe explains. "Hank'll call you in as soon as it's ready."

I try not to show how disappointed I am. The thought of running again has kept me awake nights for weeks. My heart starts racing, and I just can't seem to settle it down. Some nights I sneak downstairs to watch the YouTube clips, just to convince myself that it's not a dream, that I really am going to be able to *run*.

And now I have to wait.

Again.

But the minute I walk on my new leg, I forget about the running leg—at least for a little while.

My new leg is amazing!

It goes on a little differently than my first leg, and it uses what's called a shuttle-lock system. A suction sleeve liner goes right over my stump, and it has a two-inch notched metal peg sticking out of the bottom of it. When I put my stump into the socket, the notched peg pushes down through a hole in the base of the socket. It makes a ratchety clicking sound as it goes in, and then I'm *connected*. The suction sleeve is locked into the socket, and the combination feels snug and comfortable . . . like it belongs.

And the foot! Under the rubbery fake toes are layers of black carbon graphite that look nothing like a real foot, but the foot flexes with me and gives some bounce to my step.

"I love this!" I say after the preliminary adjustments are done. "I had no idea it would be this much better than my first one."

It still looks very Frankensteinish but more high-tech. Instead of a pipe, it's got a two-inch-wide flat, black carbon-graphite bar.

"I'm going to need you to come back for fine-tuning like you did before," Hank tells me. "And when we've got you dialed in, we'll get you a cosmetic cover." He smiles at me. "You'll be standing pretty."

I stop walking and take a good look at him. I wonder how I could ever have hated this man. Or, at least, how I could ever have been so angry with him. "Thanks," I tell him softly. "Thanks for helping me through this."

He smiles at me. "I know it seems like a lifetime to you, but you've made outstanding progress in the short time you've been coming in."

This time I feel like I deserve the compliment. I've worked hard on my gait; on learning how to adapt. And watching myself in the mirror now, I see that part of my problem was the tools I was using. The old leg was clunky compared to this one. With my new "flex foot" my gait looks smooth, my stride confident.

I feel almost . . . normal.

When we're done and his tools are put away, he walks me out. "The one thing I can't build for my clients is up here," he says, tapping his head with a finger. "No matter how good the prosthesis is, if the mind isn't willing, the leg won't work. With you I know I don't have to worry about that." He grins at me. "You're going to do and be whatever you want."

I thank him again and wave a cheery goodbye to Chloe. Then I walk out of there, this time with a spring in my step.

chapter 18

When Fiona picks me up for our movie shift that night, I'm excited to show her my new moves.

"Wow!" she says after I've done my best runway impression along our hallway. "You are *smooth*."

I laugh and do a little dance. "It's awesome."

"So, you ready?" she asks. "Do you need to say bye to your mom or anything?"

I shake my head. "She's out doing something with Kaylee, and Dad's still at work."

"Well then, let's roll."

The Tremont Theater has a little kiosk in front where tickets are sold. It *is* attached to the foyer, but it sticks way out, and tonight Greta is behind the window.

"She looks like a gypsy fortune-teller," I whisper to Fiona as we approach.

"She sure does!" Fiona says with a giggle.

But something about it is odd. Greta never actually takes a position. She more moves around the place, supervising. "I wonder what happened. She never works the window."

Fiona whispers, "She should, though, don't you think? Look at her! It would be great for business. People would come up wondering about having their fortune told, and she could sell them on the movie instead."

"Hi, girls," Greta says through the window.

"Everything okay?" I ask.

"Sure it is. Just incredibly slow is all." She waves a gnarled hand toward the entrance. "Go on. I'm sure you can find something to clean, anyway."

Fiona holds the door open for me, and when I step inside, I'm struck by how quiet it is. And empty. It's weird—there's no one behind the counter, no one ordering food, no one at all anywhere. It feels like I've stepped onto an empty movie set. Or into a wax museum. Or—

"SURPRISE!"

Heads pop up from behind everywhere, and at first I'm just *shocked*, but as I start to absorb who's there, I realize it's the track team. And Kyro. And my parents. And my sister. And Gavin. And Hank and Chloe. And Marla Sumner, along with her cameraman.

"Well, girl," Greta says from beside me, "I'd say the celebration has begun."

I turn to her. "But what about . . ."

She snorts. "Honey, the place is all yours."

Kyro's heading toward me, followed by the rest of the crowd. He's carrying an enormous rectangular box, wrapped in gold foil paper and a broad blue ribbon.

My mom's crying.

My dad is, too.

My teammates are pogoing around like maniacs, so excited to be giving me this gift.

Hank grins at me, and through my tears I tell him, "You stinker!"

Kyro hands the box over, and he's teared up, too. "Run well, Jessica."

I carry the box over to the popcorn counter, and while everyone gathers around, I unwrap my running leg.

I already know what it's going to look like. Hank and I've gone over it many times. It's going to be a black J-shaped leg with a smooth foot instead of spikes. The spikes will get added later, when I'm ready to race. It'll also have an awesome flame fabric that Fiona and I picked out, embedded in the socket.

So I *know* what it's going to look like, but that's not what I see when I open the box.

The J-shaped part is there, but there's nothing flame-like about the socket.

It's blue.

With some strange yellowish gold pattern.

My first reaction is, *This is the wrong leg.* But then I see that the strange yellow pattern is writing.

Signatures.

Comments.

Things my teammates have written.

Run, Jessica!

We love you, Jessica!

Run like the wind!

You're amazing!

Believe!

Race me!

Welcome back, Jessica!

It's a bird, it's a plane, no . . . it's Jessica Carlisle!

I can't read any more, because I'm sobbing. Fiona hands me a napkin, and I wipe my eyes and choke out, "I love you guys. What did I ever do to deserve you? Thank you so, *so* much."

I lay the leg back inside the box and hug everybody. Ev-ery-body. And while I'm hugging, I notice something that makes me feel even better.

My dad and Kyro are shaking hands, smiling.

A few minutes later Hank and Kyro make a date to meet me at the track the next day so we can figure out and fine-tune the leg, and then Greta turns on some music and we party. We eat too much popcorn, we drink too much soda, and we dance.

On two joyous feet, I dance.

PART V

Starting Line

chapter 1

My FIRST DAY WITH THE RUNNING LEG I definitely do not go out and charge over Aggery Bridge.

I can barely even walk in the thing.

It's a strange contraption. Stilty, and almost scary. It's also taller than my good leg, which Hank says it's supposed to be, but I feel off-kilter.

Completely unbalanced.

Kyro and Hank work with me on the Liberty track, but I'm afraid of the leg. It makes me feel like I'm going to fall, or trip, or crash and burn.

Plus Mom and Kaylee and Fiona and some of the track team are there, and I feel like people have really high expectations.

Expectations that I'm not even coming close to meeting.

Everyone tells me not to worry about it, but I do worry about it. People paid a lot of money to buy me this leg, and it frustrates me that I can't work it right.

Hank makes adjustments for me, but no matter what he does to it, it just doesn't feel right. My legs are so different from each other—like strangers that will never really work well together. It seems that they should either both be running legs or both be regular legs. One of each is a mismatch—one I can't get the rhythm for.

It's not until three sessions later that things start going better. This isn't a walking leg, or even a jogging leg. It's a *running* leg. And when I finally really *push* for the first time, something inside me clicks.

And bursts free.

It's like I'm a little kid again, wobbling along on my bicycle.

I'm exhilarated.

Terrified.

Gaining speed.

Sure to crash.

It's a wild, electrifying feeling, and once I get a taste of it, I'm hooked. I go out to the track every day. At first I switch legs in the car, but it's cramped and cumbersome, and I finally get the guts to walk out to the infield on my "flex foot" leg and then, in front of God and athletes and middle-aged joggers, switch to my running leg.

I'm getting good at the switch. It only takes me about ten seconds now. And I'm more comfortable with the leg; more comfortable with people's curiosity.

"That is amazing," people tell me as we share the track.

I always agree. "Yes, it is!"

I also discover something painful.

I'm out of shape!

But as every athlete knows—no pain, no gain. So I push

myself. Sometimes I run with Fiona, sometimes by myself. And sometimes I have sessions with Kyro. He has me visualize smooth running, which in some mysterious way seems to help. I haven't graduated from the track yet because even though I've been running every day for over two weeks now, Mom's not allowing me to run streets for a while. She's still worried about me tripping or slipping, and the track just seems safer to her.

So I am getting used to it, and I am gaining confidence, but I honestly don't know if I'll ever race again.

It almost doesn't matter, though.

I can *run*.

chapter 2

I HAVE THE RUNNING DREAM AGAIN.

It's early morning.

Sherlock's whole body is wagging as he dances in a circle by the front door.

We ease out, turn right when we hit the street, and head toward the river. The world is quiet. No cars. No people. No hustle and bustle. Just the rhythmic sound of our feet against pavement.

Sherlock is happy beside me. "*Aaarooo!*" he says, for no apparent reason. "*Aaarooooooo!*"

We reach the river, and the air is heavenly. Cool and moist. It sparkles my face, washes my lungs, cools the building heat of my body. I soar beneath the trees, transform into wind.

We come upon Aggery Bridge and I begin the long sprint across it. My legs and lungs burn, but I welcome this pain.

It forges me with strength.

Determination.

Triumph.

I drop back the pace now and glide along the streets, back past familiar houses, back home. The sun is brighter now, the air warmer. Sweat pours from me. Cool, salty, cleansing sweat.

On the porch again, Sherlock kisses me and pants as I tousle his ears. "Good boy!" I tell him. "You are such a good boy!"

Our sleepy neighborhood is stirring, waking up, and this time I stay on the porch with Sherlock and enjoy it.

This time there is no shock for me.

No jolt awake.

No tears.

This time, the running dream is real.

chapter 3

Now THAT MOM'S CUT ME LOOSE and I'm in good enough
shape, Sherlock and I run the whole five-mile loop over Aggery Bridge every morning. When I wake up tired, I remind
myself how long I've waited to be able to run again, and it
gets me up. Gets me moving into that plane between dreaming and reality where only running seems to take me.

Some mornings I see Rosa on her porch, and when I do, I
finish my run, then trot back to visit with her. It's a nice cool-
down for Sherlock and for me.

We talk about her online friends, and the summer courses
she's been taking online, and the places she's seen online that
she dreams about going to someday.

I start to see that the Internet is the way she travels; the
way she socializes; the way she feels like part of things.

It's the place where people see her, not her condition.

Often on my walk home, I try to think of ways to help her
live some of the things she dreams about, but I have no idea
what to do.

I feel bad, too, that she wasn't at my surprise party, and

that she wasn't asked to sign my socket. If I had known about the party, I would have made sure she was there, but even Fiona—who is the kindest, most thoughtful person on earth—didn't think about inviting her.

Rosa is . . . invisible.

She finds out about parties after they're over.

This time from a TV newscast.

She didn't pout or try to make me feel bad about the party—she was just congratulatory and happy for me. But I *did* feel bad. I *still* feel bad. She's the one who got me through Ms. Rucker's class. She helped me feel hope. She cheered me on and made me see things in ways I hadn't before. She should have been there.

And now . . . now I'm running again. I know I'll never be able to run a fifty-five flat in the 400 again. Kyro timed me at the track the other day, and I ran a seventy-one five. But that's okay. I'm happy just to be running, and I *will* work up to competing. Maybe in a longer race, like the 1600. Kyro says he'll help me find the race that's right for me, and I'm looking forward to that.

Rosa, though, is still the same. And I can see momentum pulling me out of her life. We have different interests, we're in different years in school. . . . It wouldn't be hard for her to fade into my past.

But I don't want that to happen.

I don't want Rosa to be left behind.

chapter 4

I GET THE IDEA right before I fall asleep.

And then I *can't* sleep.

I'm up half the night thinking about it, adding to it, visualizing it, wondering if it's even possible.

In all the thinking I do, I never for a minute think it's crazy, but I'm afraid my parents will. So early the next morning I put on my running leg, sneak downstairs, and find my wheelchair in the garage.

"Come on, boy," I whisper to Sherlock, and make a sly exit out the side door of the garage.

The wheelchair is small, light, easy to push. I make it to the end of the block and back no problem.

So I put a big sack of potting soil in the seat and try again.

It's already harder.

Much harder.

Okay, I tell myself, *see what you can do.*

"Let's go," I tell Sherlock, and he falls into step beside me as I push the wheelchair along the streets of our usual route toward Aggery Bridge.

It's late August, so although it's only six o'clock, the sun is already up, and the air is warming. Even before the one-mile mark I'm sweating and panting hard. My arms are straining. My legs can feel the burn. Any uphill, no matter how slight, feels ten times harder than it usually does, and it's becoming clear that I'm not going to be able to do this for the full five miles of my loop.

A little farther, I tell myself. *Then you can turn around.*

I coax myself forward with milestones:

Just to the end of the block.

Just to the stop sign.

Just to the next bend.

My arms are tired of holding the handles.

I want to let go.

I want to stop.

But I press on.

Just to the next intersection.

Just to the moving van.

Just to the top of the rise.

I feel a hot spot forming on my stump—a warning sign Hank has told me I should pay close attention to.

Blisters, he says, can set me back weeks.

"Jessica!"

I'm hearing my name, but I'm not.

"Jessica! Hey!"

I slow, then stop and turn to face the sound.

A man is waving at me from across the street.

He's tan. Lean. Handsome.

He's wearing running shorts. A sweat-drenched T-shirt.

And as he crosses over, I'm thinking, *It can't be him*, but then there it is—chin scruff.

"Gavin?" I'm suddenly aware how odd it is to be running with a load of potting soil in a wheelchair.

He laughs. "What are you doing?"

"Uh . . ." I follow his gaze to the wheelchair. "Hard to explain."

He doesn't press. "Okay . . . well, you want some company? I could run with you."

"Uh . . . actually, I was getting ready to turn around. I usually do a loop, but I'm not going to make five miles pushing this thing. I'm already wiped out."

"So I'll run back with you."

I turn the wheelchair around. "Don't feel like you have to watch over the crazy girl pushing a load of potting soil. I'll be fine."

And then, out of the blue, he asks, "Do I bug you, or what?"

My head snaps to face him. "What are you talking about?"

"You always seem like you're trying to get away from me."

"I *do*?"

"Yeah. I'll think that we're having a good time and then you'll practically ditch me."

"Wow. I'm sorry. I didn't mean it like that."

"Then what?"

I start jogging, and he stays right beside me, a heavy silence between us. Finally I say, "Look. You've been really nice, and really helpful, but I don't want you to do things for me or pay attention to me because you feel sorry for me."

He's quiet a minute. "Is that what you think?"

"Kinda, yeah." And I want to add, I also think you've got a secret crush on Fiona, but I'm already feeling bad for what I *did* say. "Look," I finally say. "I'm sorry. I—"

"I made that mistake once, okay? I sure wouldn't do it again."

"You made—" I glance at him. "What are you talking about?"

"Does the name Merryl ring a bell?"

We run along in silence for a bit. "Are you saying . . ."

"We broke up." He shakes his head. "It was just a mistake. She was a mess at Lucy's funeral, and I got caught up in feeling sorry for her. But it was a terrible reason to go out with her."

"Sorry to hear that," I say softly, because really, I don't know what else to say.

"And of course I felt sorry for you, but . . ." He stops running. "Didn't you read what I wrote on your running leg? Does it say, *I feel sorry for you*? No! It says, *You inspire me*. I want to be around you because you inspire me! You're amazing. I think you're the most . . ."

I stop running, and I look at him.

His hair is pressed off his forehead and sticking out at the sides. His T-shirt is still soaked, and he's covered in sweat.

He is gorgeous.

". . . incredible person . . ."

And I *did* read what he wrote on my running leg. I read it over and over and over.

". . . I have ever known."

He's looking at me, too, but he doesn't seem to be looking at my hair, which is surely a mess, or thinking about the sweat I'm covered in.

He's just looking into my eyes.

"So what are you saying?" I ask meekly.

He looks at me a few moments longer, then answers with a long, salty kiss.

chapter 5

SHERLOCK BARKS, howls, and spins in a circle.

I pull away and laugh, then tell Gavin, "He's saying, 'You kissed a one-legged girl who's pushing around a wheelchair with potting soil in it!'"

He looks at Sherlock. "And she kissed me back!" He turns to me, and he's smiling. Really smiling. "So . . . does this mean you don't think I'm annoying?"

I shake my head, and as we start walking toward my house, I let him push the wheelchair and tell him, "I've actually been trying hard *not* to like you. Besides, I was sure you had a thing for Fiona."

"For Fiona?" He lets that sink in. "No wonder you were always ditching me."

So we talk and catch up and confess all sorts of silly things, and when we're on my street, he says, "So is this wheelchair thing to build up your strength? Running with this would not be easy."

"No. Well, yeah, I guess so." I shake my head a little. "I just had this idea, but now I don't think it'll work."

"So what's the idea?"

And in that moment I decide to tell him. "You know Rosa, right?"

"Of course."

"Well, she lives around the corner from me. On Marigold?"

"Okay . . ."

"It's a long story, but she sits out on her porch in the mornings and sees me run by. I go back and talk to her and . . . well, she asks me about running a lot. Why I do it, what it feels like . . . and she has this thing about the finish line."

"About the finish line? What do you mean?"

"I don't know exactly, but she's very philosophical about it. I think she sees it as this amazing moment . . . one she'll never experience."

He raises an eyebrow at the wheelchair. "So you're . . . You want to get her over a finish line?"

"I don't know. First I thought about just taking her on my loop . . . but then the idea grew into maybe I could do the River Run with her in November. Kyro had the team volunteer last year during cross-country—we handed out cups of Gatorade and water at the mile stations—and there were wheelchair racers and lots of people running for causes." I shrug. "I thought it would be the perfect run for Rosa."

"That's a ten-mile run," he says quietly.

"I know. But it's the only one around here." I frown. "But after today I don't think I'm going to be able to do it." I eye the wheelchair. "That's *maybe* twenty-five pounds? Rosa's small, but she's got to weigh close to a hundred." I shake my head. "I didn't even make it two miles."

"But this was your first try?" When I nod, he adds, "And look at this wheelchair. It's a toy compared to some of the ones I've seen. Maybe if you had a chair with bigger wheels. One that was designed for racing?"

We're standing at my walkway now. I love the serious look on his face; how he's trying to find ways to make this work.

"And how long have you been running again? A month?"

"Not quite."

"See? Like you've even had a chance to build up your own strength?"

I think about this a moment. "So don't throw in the towel?"

"Give it a chance." He thinks, too, then asks, "Does she know about this?"

"Rosa? No. I haven't told anyone. I wanted to see if it was even possible."

He smiles and reaches out for my hand. "So you want to try again tomorrow? I'll meet you here at, what, six?"

"Are you serious?"

He pulls me in closer. "Sure."

I laugh and I smile and I look into his eyes and see my little idea blooming inside him. Suddenly I feel stronger.

Like maybe this isn't so crazy.

In this moment, *anything* seems possible.

chapter 6

AFTER GAVIN LEAVES, I run inside to call Fiona, but there's a slight problem:

My dad has seen everything.

He doesn't *say* this exactly, but from the arch of his eyebrow and his position in the family room, I know he has.

I face him, wondering how to explain.

The boy . . . the wheelchair . . . the potting soil . . . there's a lot to explain!

But I'm feeling really *happy,* and what's to hide?

So I sit down and start.

First with the boy.

"His name's Gavin Vance. He's the one who wrote that newspaper article about me. I've had a crush on him for ages."

This is received with a single nod.

One of cautionary approval.

And then, being in a heady, sharing sort of mood, I explain the wheelchair, the potting soil, and Rosa, like it's all perfectly normal.

There's no nod for this part, just a knit brow and a dubious frown.

Mom enters the room and asks what's going on, and after Dad and I exchange looks, I explain everything all over again.

The part about Rosa and the River Run doesn't actually sink in because she's completely fixated on Gavin.

"So . . . is he your *boyfriend?*"

"I don't know." I give a little laugh and a shrug. "But we have a date to go running with a wheelchair and potting soil tomorrow at six."

"AM?" she asks.

I grin. "Yup."

"Does that count as a date?"

I shrug. "Does to me!"

She looks to Dad for his opinion, but Dad's been thinking about something else.

The wheelchair.

"I don't want to say you'll never make it ten miles with your friend in that wheelchair, but it'll be slightly less impossible if you let me put some better wheels on it. And I'm sure she'd appreciate a more comfortable seat."

"Huh?" My brain shifts from Gavin to the River Run. "Really? That would be great!"

He nods. "Let me talk to Ed at the Bike Barn—get his advice. I'll be out that way on a job this morning."

I go over and hug him. "You are the best!" I pull back and look at him. "I don't tell you that enough, do I?" I hug him again. Tight. "You are the *best*."

"Well," he says, and he's smiling, "I like the mood this Gavin fella has put you in, that's for sure." He kisses me on the temple and says, "Now I'd better get to work."

Mom walks him out, and before she can return to cross-examine me, I've escaped to my room with my cell phone. News like this can't wait for a "reasonable hour."

I've got to talk to Fiona!

chapter 7

THE LAST DAYS OF SUMMER BREAK are some of the best of my life. Gavin runs with Sherlock and me in the mornings, and then Fiona, Mario, Gavin, and I spend time together when we can—at the park, or in Old Town, or just hanging out at a coffee shop, talking and laughing about nothing and everything.

Cross-country practice has already begun, and although I can't go out for the team this year because most of the race-courses are over uneven terrain, dirt hills, or gravel paths where my running leg's not designed to go, I run laps around the track and continue to do speed work. I race the straight-aways, then jog the curves. Or I sprint a 200, then jog a 200. Or if the team's doing street work, I join them for that. For most of us, cross-country is what we do to build up our base for track. Kyro unofficially requires it unless you're doing another fall sport, and although I was never a fan of distance running before, Kyro's "you're on your honor to run this weekend" is what got me into running the Aggery Bridge loop.

So I've been working hard and improving at a pretty good rate. I'm up to at least eight miles a day, five of them with the wheelchair—a wheelchair that my dad's made much easier to push. It now has big wheels, a padded seat, and a broader footrest, plus a serious seat belt and a hand brake for safety. He's also welded a crossbar between the handles so I can push one-handed if my arms need a break.

He didn't stop there, either. He replaced the potting soil with twenty-five-pound sandbags, got me bike gloves for my hands—which are a lifesaver—and added pouches to the sides for water bottles, which is something I've really needed in this heat.

I also got a good tip from Hank—I put antiperspirant on my stump. I was sweating and getting hot spots on my leg, having to dry out my liner mid-run to keep from getting blisters. The antiperspirant has really helped.

I've been avoiding Rosa's house because I didn't want her to know what I was planning until I was sure I could do it. I'm still not sure that I can—not even close to sure—but my mom brought up a good point: "What if her mother doesn't want you to do this?"

So the Saturday before school starts I finally decide that it's time, and I jog over to Rosa's house with Sherlock and the wheelchair.

Rosa sees me coming. "Jessica!" she calls through the screen door. It's only ten in the morning, but it's already eighty degrees out—a good day to stay inside. "Hey, what's that?" she asks, motoring out onto the porch.

"Is your mom here?" I ask.

"Mo-om!" she calls over her shoulder, then turns back to my wheelchair. "Who built that? What's in the seat? Where are you going?"

Rosa's mom is on the porch now, too. "Hello, Jessica! Do you want to come in? It's awfully warm out here."

"Uh, no. I just need to ask you something."

Rosa shakes her head. "All of us are asking questions! Who's got answers?"

I smile at her. "I do. To answer yours first . . . my dad retrofitted my wheelchair so I could run with it."

"You *run* with that?" Rosa asks.

I nod. "And what's in the seat is one twenty-five-pound sandbag, and"—I pick up the white kitchen trash liner that's next to it—"two five-pound sacks of flour."

They both look at me like I've got sunstroke.

I laugh, but I'm suddenly feeling very foolish. I focus on Rosa. "You know how you ask me about running? How you talk about the finish line? How it's some mystical thing that you wish you could experience?"

Her eyes are growing wide.

"Well, I've been running with this almost every day, adding weight to it, trying to build up to—"

"Really?" she asks, and her eyes are enormous. "You're going to run *me* in that?"

"What are you saying?" her mom asks, and there's definitely concern in her voice.

"Well . . . I'm thinking Rosa and I could do the River Run together. It's a ten-mile race, which is long, but it's the only community run around here. It's in November, so I have about two months to build up my endurance. But before I go any further with my training, I thought I should make sure it's okay with you. And make sure Rosa wants to do it."

"Yes! I absolutely want to!" Rosa squeals from her seat. "Yes!"

Mrs. Brazzi seems very skeptical.

"My dad's put on big tires and a padded seat to make the ride comfortable, plus there's a wide seat belt and a hand brake for safety." I feel like a used-car salesman, and Mrs. Brazzi is looking at me like I *am* one. "I promise I'll be safe," I tell her.

"Please, Mom?" Rosa asks.

Mrs. Brazzi sighs, then looks at me. "It's you pushing, right? No one else?"

I nod.

She looks at her daughter.

Looks at me.

Looks at the chair.

Finally she sighs again and says, "If this is what you girls want . . ."

"Awesome!" Rosa cries. Then she looks at me with wide eyes and says, "Can we try it now?"

I think about it, then give a little shrug. "You probably ought to try out the chair and see how it feels."

So while she powers down the porch ramp in her motorized wheelchair, I remove the sacks of flour and the sandbag from the running wheelchair. Then Rosa locks her wheels and does a transfer. She's wobbly on her legs, and they won't really support her, but the transfer is actually very smooth.

Her mother fusses with the safety belt and says to Rosa, "I'm going to get you a helmet."

"No!" Rosa cries. "No helmet!"

Rosa says it so forcefully that Mrs. Brazzi and I are both startled.

"I don't want to be the weird kid in the helmet," Rosa says quietly. "And I want to feel the wind."

I think back. How many times have I told Rosa about facing into the wind; cutting into the wind; *feeling* the wind run cool fingers through your hair?

More than I can count.

"Believe me," I say to Mrs. Brazzi, "I won't be going that fast."

She considers all this, then heaves another sigh. "Okay, then."

"Thank you, Mom!" Rosa cries. "Oh, thank you!"

So I push off and run Rosa around the block.

One short block.

Rosa's mother is waiting on the sidewalk when we return, and Rosa is ecstatic, bubbling about how much fun it is.

Me, I'm pouring sweat and exhausted. I want to yank off my leg and jump in the mermaid fountain.

It was only one block.

One short block.

Rosa and her mother have both come on board with this, but now I do seriously wonder about the sanity of it.

If one block was this hard, how will I ever make ten miles?

chapter 8

THERE REALLY IS NO BACKING OUT NOW.

Gavin, Fiona, Mario, Mom, Dad, Kaylee . . . they all tell me everyone will understand if I decide it's too hard, but I can't quit now.

I just can't.

So I confide in Kyro, and I ask him to help me. "I need to get strong enough to do this," I tell him after school is back in session.

We're in his classroom, and I watch as his strong, graceful hands sort stacks of papers, clipping them into groups as he thinks.

Finally he says, "Pushing close to a hundred pounds . . . plus the weight of the wheelchair . . . that would be hard for an able-bodied person."

"Hey! I'm able-bodied."

He eyes me. "You know what I mean." Then he adds, "And more important, it's the weight. How much do you weigh, Jessica? One twenty? One thirty?"

With or without my leg?

I just shrug.

"So you're pushing close to your own weight over ten miles."

"Look," I tell him, "I'm going to do it. I'm asking you to help me."

He holds my gaze for a long moment, then nods. "Okay." He turns to his calendar. "What are we looking at? Eight weeks? And what are you up to?"

"The River Run is the first weekend in November. I did five miles with forty pounds this morning."

"Plus the wheelchair?"

I nod.

"And what was your level of effort?"

"It was hard," I admit.

He nods again. "Okay. I'll work up a schedule. And we've got to get you into the weight room. And on a muscle-building diet." He eyes me, but there's a twinkle behind the seriousness. "You thought the four hundred was bad?"

I laugh, but I know I'm in for it.

And that's okay.

It's the only way I'll get Rosa over that finish line.

chapter 9

I STICK TO KYRO'S PLAN. I alternate running and lifting. I'm sore a lot. I ice my legs after hard runs. I hydrate the way he wants me to. I eat a lot of tuna. I take good care of my stump, watching for hot spots, avoiding chafing and blisters.

I add another sandbag to the wheelchair.

Guys in the weight room eventually accept me; eventually quit staring at my leg. I go in, work out, sweat buckets, and get out. I focus on the goal. Focus on Rosa's happiness. Focus on the finish line.

Gavin runs with me when he can, and we do our homework together almost every night. Kaylee's a freshman now, and very impressed that my boyfriend is Gavin Vance. "He's, like, *popular*," she tells me one night.

I laugh. "Yeah. Unbelievable, huh?"

And then one Saturday afternoon I'm doing a long, slow distance run without the wheelchair when a funny thing happens.

A stranger calls out my name.

"Jessica!"

I'm near Old Town, familiarizing myself with the River Run route, and when I turn, I see a woman with her two children waving at me from across the street.

"You're Jessica!" she calls.

I laugh and wave. "Yes, I am!"

"Good for you!" she calls back. "Congratulations!"

"Thank you!" I shout, and continue running.

This buoys me through my run, and after this first time, it happens almost every time I run. People call to me from cars, wave at me from bridges, shout, "Run, Jessica!" from across the street . . . somehow the word has spread through our little town that the one-legged girl is running again.

As I run, I wonder how many of these people helped buy my leg.

I wonder about the deep, wide abyss between good intentions and concrete action, and how many of them leapt across it.

Is that why they're so happy to see me run?

Because they helped make it happen?

Or are they just happy to see the girl they read about in the paper—the one they saw peg-leg around on TV—running again?

Either way, I find their enthusiasm to be contagious. It helps me press on. Helps me add weight to the wheelchair. And when they ask why I'm pushing sandbags in a wheelchair, I'm happy to tell them about Rosa and the River Run. "Wish me luck!" I always say, and they do.

I get a lot of thumbs-ups.

I give a lot of thumbs-ups back.

Some weekends Gavin joins Sherlock and me on my distance run. He's offered since the beginning to take turns pushing the wheelchair, but I made a deal with Mrs. Brazzi, and besides, this is something *I* want to do for Rosa.

Then Fiona and Mario decide they want to join us, and as my entourage grows, so do the cheers.

"Man!" Mario says one Saturday after about the tenth Go, Jessica. "This is crazy!"

But as much as I like the encouragement, something about it bothers me. And after it happens again, I tell the others, "This is supposed to be about Rosa, not me."

"But you're the one doing it," Fiona says.

I slow down, then stop. I'm pushing seventy-five pounds, and all of a sudden I've had enough.

"You okay?" Gavin asks.

I shake my head. "I probably spend too much time thinking about this, but in my mind this is more than just a run *for* Rosa. It's a run *about* Rosa. You know . . . like a coming-out party? Where we can say, Hey, this is our friend Rosa. Pay attention, people. She's a really great person, and a math genius, too!" As we walk along, I tell them about Rosa's notes and what she wrote about wishing people could see her, not her condition. "I want people to see *her*. I want it to be a really special day for *her*."

Gently, Gavin tells me, "But if you're our town celebrity—which it looks like you are—you're the one who will bring the attention to Rosa. You're the one who will help people see Rosa. If I pushed her, it wouldn't have the same impact as it will when you do it."

Everyone's quiet for about half a block, and then Fiona says, "Remember last year at the River Run when Kyro had us passing out Gatorade? There were runners who had their names on their shirts? And complete strangers would shout their names as they ran by? Maybe we can make CHEER FOR ROSA or TEAM ROSA shirts?"

Leave it to Fiona to come up with something brilliant.

I look at her and smile. "Team Rosa—I love that idea!"

"We could do signs or flags . . . tall ones!" She's thinking a mile a minute. "We could strap them to the wheelchair and—"

"Oh, nice," I tell her. "Increase my wind resistance."

She ignores me and my increased wind resistance. "Gavin, Mario, and I could toot horns, or shake clappers, or—"

"Oh. I'm going so slow you've got the energy to toot horns?"

She faces me. "You're pushing a hundred pounds!"

I laugh, and say, "And you're willing to wear silly shirts and toot horns and carry flags for ten miles?"

But what's silly, really, is my question.

"I'm in," she says, putting her hand out, palm down.

"Me too," Mario says, putting his hand on top of hers.

"So am I," Gavin says, piling on.

I add my hand to the stack, and Sherlock seals the deal with a happy "Aaaroooo!"

Team Rosa is official.

chapter 10

SOMEONE CALLS CHANNEL 7.

Marla Sumner calls me.

"Why didn't you tell me you were doing this?" she asks. "This is an amazing story!"

I agree to her doing a story, but I have one condition: "The focus needs to be on Rosa."

Still. The process leaves me very uncomfortable. Marla starts out at Rosa's house, but after the initial interview there, the news crew follows me everywhere. On a run with the wheelchair, driving to school with Fiona, in the weight room with football players, on the track with Kyro . . . the focus definitely does not feel like it's on Rosa.

Finally, when Marla asks me, "What do you think about when you run?" I snap.

"Look," I tell her, "this is not about me. I'm doing this for Rosa. And yeah, at first I just wanted her to experience a run—to cross a finish line and hear people cheering for her—because that's something she wanted. But you know what? Her biggest wish isn't to cross a finish line or have people cheer for her. It's to have people see *her* instead of her condition. That's all anybody with a disability wants. Don't sum up the person based on what you see, or what you don't understand; get to know *them*."

She packs up quickly after that, and I feel a little bad for having snapped, because I know she means well. But the truth is, I'm glad she's gone.

Then Friday night when the story airs, I discover that Marla Sumner has put her own spin on things.

"Jessica Carlisle is back on two feet, and this time she's running for a cause."

My mom and dad look at me, and I give them a wide-eyed shrug.

"She's not raising money," Marla states. "She's raising awareness."

"I am?" I ask the televised Marla.

And then she launches into the story. They asked Rosa and me to mock up a tutoring session, and this is the footage Marla's voice speaks over. "Rosa Brazzi was born with cerebral palsy, a condition caused by damage to the motor control centers of a developing brain. Similar to a stroke, cerebral palsy can occur during pregnancy, childbirth, or up to the age of about three, and although there is a broad range in how CP can affect a person, in Rosa's case her motor functions have been hindered but her brain is as sharp as they come."

The camera is on me now. "She's a math genius!" I say with a laugh. "I would never have made it through algebra without her help!"

"And since one good turn deserves another," Marla's

voice is saying, "Jessica Carlisle wants to help Rosa do something she would never be able to do on her own—go for a run."

"When Jessica runs me," Rosa says, "I feel like I'm flying."

Now there's footage of Rosa in the running wheelchair as I push her down the block. "The goal," Marla's voice says, "is to cross the River Run finish line this November." The shot swings around to behind us running, zeroing in on my right leg. "But for a young woman with a handicap of her own, pushing one hundred pounds along ten miles is not something that can be done on a whim."

Now there's a series of clips of me—running with the sandbags through Old Town, waving at the garbage collector as he calls my name, working in the weight room at school, and doing speed work on the track. All of it has Marla's commentary over it.

Then she asks, "So what, in a nutshell, is the cause Jessica and Rosa are running for? Quite simply, it's to have people see them, not their condition."

And then there's the footage of me saying, "That's all anybody with a disability wants. Don't sum up the person based on what you see, or what you don't understand; get to know *them*."

Then they switch back to the studio, where Marla and Kevin are behind the news desk.

"The River Run is in two short weeks," Marla says, looking into the camera as she winds up the story. "We'll be there live, and we hope you'll join us in cheering for Rosa."

"And Jessica!" Kevin adds.

Marla smiles. "They're quite a team."

After the TV's clicked off, Mom stares at me.

Dad stares at me.

Kaylee, who's been texting the whole time, says, "I thought you were crazy before, but I get it now."

And I stare at *her*, because the funny thing is, that's exactly how I feel.

chapter 11

I KNOW WHERE THE GRAVEYARD IS.

I can see the taller grave markers from one of the streets on the River Run route.

Sometimes if I'm concentrating on my form or my time, I don't notice that I've run past it, but today I'm not thinking about those things.

I'm thinking about Lucy.

I turn off the main street and find the graveyard entrance. It's Sunday mid-morning, and the air is still cool and crisp, but the bordering trees have left a carpet of leaves beneath them. Reds, browns, yellows . . . they give the grounds a warm, cozy look.

I park the wheelchair beside a tree and keep Sherlock at heel as we wander among the graves. It takes me some time, but I find her.

LUCY SANDERS
OUR ANGEL

"Hi, Lucy," I begin. "It's me, Jessica."
But I've never spoken to a grave before.

I don't know what to say.

I don't know how.

"I'm so sorry," I choke out, but that's as far as I get before I start crying. I feel bad that she's gone. I feel overwhelmed. And I feel guilt.

Guilt that I've recovered.

Guilt that I'm happy.

Guilt that I ever thought she was the lucky one.

I can't get the words out, so I just cry.

"Jessica?"

The voice startles me. It's soft, female, and seems to be right in my ear.

But it's not the ghost of Lucy, it's a woman.

At first I think it's someone who's seen me on TV, and I want to snap, Leave me alone! Can't you see I'm crying here? But then I realize that I do know her.

She's more gray and frail, but I recognize her from last year's track meets.

And she *is* carrying flowers.

"Mrs. Sanders?"

She gives me a warm smile. "It's so nice of you to remember Lucy."

"Oh, I'll never forget Lucy," I say, and a new flood of tears comes forward.

She wraps an arm around me. "Aren't you sweet." Then, after I've composed myself a little, she smiles again and says, "Your father has been very helpful."

"He has?" I ask.

She nods. "We would never have had the strength to pursue a settlement without him." She strokes my arm. "Your

311

situation is more complicated, I know, but it looks like we've reached an agreement. We're thinking about setting up a scholarship fund in Lucy's name—something like that."

"Oh," I say, nodding, "that would be nice."

"Congratulations on your recovery," she says. "I see you on the news a lot!"

"Thanks," I say softly.

And after a few more pleasantries, I leave so she can deliver the flowers she's brought and talk to her daughter in peace.

chapter 12

SCHOOL SEEMS ALMOST EASY THIS YEAR. Not having math helps, but I think that anything would feel easy compared to last year. There's no work to make up—I just have to keep up.

Plus now that I'm walking on my new leg, people really do seem to forget that there's something different about me.

I'm still very aware of it, but other people treat me like I'm normal.

The big exception is Merryl.

I'm in two classes with her, and she always gives me the evil eye from afar. I try to ignore her, but it's a little unnerving to have someone stare at you that hard for that long.

She's on her third boyfriend since Gavin, so I don't know what her problem is with me, but today she actually comes up to me.

"He's only going out with you because he feels sorry for you," she whispers as she invades my personal space on a classroom ramp. "You're, like, his community service project."

I'm stunned, and the truth is, her comments cut deep.

I have no zinger to fire back.

I just watch as she hurries away.

Later when I tell Fiona about it, she grabs me by the arm and says, "Do *not* even for a *second* believe that! She's just shallow and insanely jealous. Not to mention cruel."

I hear her words, but Merryl's voice still echoes in my head.

Finally I break down and tell Gavin, who's sweet and comforting and assures me that there's absolutely no truth to it.

Still.

It's disturbing how fast weeds take root in my garden of worthiness.

They're so hard to pull.

And grow back so easily.

chapter 13

It's Thursday, three days before the River Run.

According to Kyro's workout schedule, I'm supposed to be "tapering"—doing easier, shorter runs—but I'm starting to panic. I just don't feel ready.

After school Kyro sends the cross-country runners off through the back hills, so I stay on the track alone. "How are you feeling?" he asks me as I'm stretching out after some warm-up laps. "You ready for the big day?"

"No," I confess. "Actually, I'm worried that I'm going to let everyone down. I can do the ten miles, but the farthest I've pushed a hundred pounds is five. And five was *hard*."

"You'll be fine," he assures me. "I'm not saying it'll be *easy*, but race-day magic will carry you through."

I shake my head. "Race-day magic?"

"You'll see. And the whole team will be out at the water stations—they'll keep you moving and get you anything you need."

I shake out my arms. I know it's from nervous energy, because it's what I used to do before getting down in the blocks for a 400-meter race. I shake them out some more. In three days I'll be facing over sixteen *thousand* meters.

Suddenly Rigor Mortis Bend doesn't seem so daunting.

It's as though Kyro can read my mind. "You need to unload some of that nervous energy. Why don't you take a lap?"

So I start down the straightaway. I'm the only runner on the track, and after the first hundred meters I find a rhythm. I don't push, I just . . . glide. It's taken some time, but I've gotten used to the sound from my running foot and the way it's paired with the quieter swish of my natural foot—*whing, whoosh, whing, whoosh.* The cadence of it is pleasant to me now, and this spin around the track feels easy.

Heavenly.

I join Kyro at our unofficial start and re-enter the real world. "Watch your arms," he says. "They're crossing over."

I laugh. "You are such a coach, Coach. I was just cruisin'."

He eyes me. And it seems like he wants to say something, but he's holding back. Finally he says, "Well, don't forget your form. Bad habits are easy to find and hard to break."

I scoff.

"You laugh? Okay, well, give me a real one this time."

"You're serious?" I ask.

"Sure." He draws a line in the dirt with his heel. "Let me see some good form."

He's being silly, but he's my coach, and since the last lap around the track felt so good, I take a few minutes to fully recover, then step up to the line. "Runners, take your mark," I announce, doing a friendly little mock of him, "set . . . *pow.*"

Whing, whoosh, whing, whoosh . . . I start down the stretch, my arms pumping. *Good form, smooth form, glide, glide,* I say inside my head.

My breathing's easy.

My rhythm's good.

I push.

Pump.

Focus.

Whing, whoosh, whing, whoosh . . .

My peripheral vision vanishes. It's all tunnel vision now.

Whing, whoosh, whing, whoosh . . .

My hands open as I pump my arms. They slice the air. Open a channel for me. Cut me through space.

Whing, whoosh, whing, whoosh . . .

I keep in form and push toward the second curve.

Whing, whoosh, whing, whoosh . . .

I approach Rigor Mortis Bend and push through it. My legs burn, but there's still power in them.

Lots of power.

Whing, whoosh, whing, whoosh . . .

I sprint for the finish line, keeping my arms pumping straight and my legs in line, and just for show I cross with a little lean forward.

I wind down, then trot back to Kyro. "So?" I ask. "Any bad habits we need to break?"

His head shakes slightly from side to side, but he's looking at me funny, and his dark skin seems pale.

"You okay?" I ask.

"You're not even breathing hard," he says quietly.

I notice he's right—I've already largely recovered.

"Well," I laugh, "it's not like it was a *race* or anything."

"Exactly," he says. "No blocks, no competition . . ." He produces a stopwatch from inside his Windbreaker pocket. The Lucy bracelet is still around his wrist. Faded and frayed, but still there.

"You clocked me?"

"After that first lap, I was curious. You seemed really strong."

"I'd better be strong," I say with a laugh. "I've got to push a hundred pounds ten miles on Sunday!"

"Well, all that training has made you *really* strong." He holds the watch out toward me, demanding that I look. "You just ran a sixty point two without even trying."

I blink at the digits. "Wow."

His face has its color back. And there's a mischievous grin forming that quickly turns into a laugh.

A deep, wonderful laugh.

One I haven't heard in ages.

One that means he's got plans for track season.

Big plans.

chapter 14

IT'S RACE DAY.

Or more like *run* day—I don't care about my time, I just want to finish.

The air is perfect—clear and crisp, but not too cold.

We're all a little nervous, penned up in the holding area, but it's a good nervous. There's an awesome vibe in the air. Runners warming up, sipping coffee, chatting.

It's seven in the morning, but everyone here is *awake*.

I'm anxious to get going, but we still have fifteen minutes to wait. Kyro's plan had me not run at all for two days, and now I'm champing at the bit.

My body needs to run.

My nerves need something to *do*.

Gavin hugs me and laughs. "You're like a filly at the starting gate!" I whinny, which makes him laugh again. He looks into my eyes and smiles. "This is the most amazing day ever, you know that? I can't believe you're here. I can't believe *I'm* here." He moves an arm out. "Look at all these people!"

I laugh, because he's definitely got race-day fever.

Or maybe this is what Kyro meant by "race-day magic"—it's just exciting to be here.

There don't seem to be any other teens in the holding area. Some college kids, maybe, but it's mostly adults, and some of them are gnarled and weathered seniors. Tough old birds!

"I'm a palindrome!" Rosa says about her 393 race number. She looks cozy in the wheelchair, with a turtleneck under her T-shirt, mittens on her hands, and a blanket over her lap.

I laugh and flash her my 369 race bib. "Yeah, and I'm a magical mathematical progression."

I've never had a race bib before, but I like it.

I've also never had a timing chip strapped to my shoe, but I like it, too.

They make me feel official.

Best of all, though, I like our T-shirts. Kyro helped Fiona with them, and they came out great. They're white, with big maroon letters that say ROOT FOR ROSA on the front and TEAM ROSA on the back.

Rosa's is a little different—hers says HELLO! I'M ROSA.

Kyro informed us that all the cross-country helpers are wearing TEAM ROSA shirts today. "They'll also have energy gels for you at the water stops," he told me. "Be smart—stay hydrated and keep your fuel up."

Fiona and the others decided against carrying signs, but they did make pendant flags for the wheelchair that say ROOT FOR ROSA and THANK YOU!

Our setup looks awesome!

Plus the boys and Rosa have clappers, and Fiona's got a horn.

We definitely look like a celebration.

"I'll be right back," Mario says, handing his clapper to Fiona as he heads off to wait in a Porta-Potty line.

Fiona shakes her head because it's his fourth trip since we arrived.

"He's nervous?" I ask, and suddenly I'm thinking I could use a trip to the bathroom myself.

But there's a woman approaching us. She's wearing a TEAM ROSA shirt, but she's not a cross-country runner.

She's a math teacher.

"Ms. Rucker?" Fiona and I say together.

She's wearing running shorts and tightly laced yellow-and-black Sauconys.

And a racing bib.

Number 27.

But it's her bare legs that are somehow shocking to see.

"Hi, girls," she says. "I just wanted to wish you good luck."

"You're a *runner*?" Fiona asks.

Ms. Rucker gives her a little shrug. "In my private life, yes."

"Wow," Fiona says.

I'm noticing Ms. Rucker's watch—it's a serious runner's watch. And her shorts have little pouches built in—I can see the tops of energy gels peeking out from both sides of her hips.

I wonder how she calculates her pace—with her watch or with her brain.

I wonder if she thinks in numbers the whole way.

If she counts her steps.

But despite all the indications that she's a machine, her shirt isn't made of that fancy sweat-wicking technical fabric that would be on par with the rest of her gear.

It's cotton, and more than just a little too big.

"Thanks for wearing the T-shirt," I tell her.

She smiles, first at me, then at Rosa.

It's an amazing sight.

Warm, and a little bit shy.

"Proud to wear it," she says, then moves away. "Run strong," she says. "I'll see you at the finish line."

I watch her go.

Run strong. . . .

I decide right then that that'll be my mantra for this race.

"All runners to the start!" someone announces over a portable PA. "Five minutes!"

Gavin checks his watch and says, "Maybe I should hunt down Mario?"

We crane our necks, checking the Porta-Potty lines. And after another minute of waiting, we're getting really antsy. Everyone in the holding area is moving toward the street.

Then suddenly, there he is. "Sorry!" he says. "We ready?"

Fiona laughs. "Yea-ah."

"Let's go!" Gavin says, leading us toward the street.

"This is so exciting!" Rosa says as I roll her along.

I laugh, because we're all like little windup toys, straining at the springs.

A runner calls, "Go, Rosa!" as he jogs by us.

"Thanks!" she calls back. Then she looks over her shoulder and says, "Go, Jessica!"

We position ourselves at the back of the pack, near a group of men wearing grass hats, with hula skirts over their running shorts.

"One minute!" the announcer calls.

My heart speeds up.

I feel suddenly light-headed.

And then there's the pop of the starting gun.

It's time.

chapter 15

IT'S THE STRANGEST START to a race I've ever experienced.

There's no shooting from the blocks, no arm pumping, no push or strain. There are hundreds of runners in front of us, and we're barely even *jogging* as we move forward. It takes nearly two minutes for us to reach the starting mat.

The mat is broad and rubbery, runs the full width of the street, and makes a chirping sound as it recognizes each runner's timing chip.

Chirp, chirp, chirp, chirp, chirp . . . It's like hyperactive twittering of mechanical chicks.

And then we're off.

I know, from having run the course in training, that the first two miles are slightly downhill, which makes the beginning of the run really enjoyable. People cheer for us, and Rosa waves and clacks her clappers in the air and calls, "Hi!" and "Thank you!"

I see Mom and Dad and Kaylee and Sherlock at the sidelines, and Kyro is there, too, cheering us on.

"You are doing *great*," Gavin says at the two-mile mark. He's checking his watch. "Nine thirty splits."

I know this is way too fast, but I feel great and figure we'll slow down now that the downhill is behind us. "Splits," I snort, then grin at him. "You have become such a runner." I lean forward a bit. "How are you doing, Rosa?"

"Great! Who knew I could run this fast!" she says with a laugh. She looks over her shoulder. "I am loving this! How are you?"

"Great!" I call back, and it's true—I feel amazing.

The course is basically U-shaped. It starts near the River Outlets, then passes by retail shops and commercial properties before moving through newer residential developments, older houses, farmland, and then just fields.

The halfway point is the Queensland Drawbridge, which arches over the river, and then the course winds back toward the historic settlement houses and into Old Town. The finish is about half a mile past Old Town.

Since I've run the route during training, I know—the easiest stretch is behind us. I need to conserve. And in the back of my mind I'm saying, *Slow down. There's no way you should be running nine thirties.*

But I don't *want* to slow down.

I am having a great time.

The crowds are thick—people are cheering like crazy.

For Rosa, and for me.

"There she is! There's that girl!"

"Go, Jessica! Go, Rosa!"

Mario and Gavin flap their clappers through the air, and Fiona toots her horn. "Thank you!" Rosa calls back, and waves like she's in a parade.

Which I guess, in a way, she is.

As we pass through the residential section, the crowds thin out. There are only small pockets of people now. They call from their porches or stand on the sidewalks and tell runners, "You're looking good! You're doing great! Keep it up!"

Then the small pockets of people vanish as we run along the road through farmland. There are some cows, but they don't moo, let alone cheer.

At first it's very picturesque. The course has leveled out, the trees are lovely, and the river looks serene. But I'm very relieved to spot our mile-four pit crew, and it worries me.

Why am I this fatigued?

It's Linzy Griggs and Shandall Norwood at the water station, and Linzy is bouncing up and down in her TEAM ROSA T-shirt. "There they are! There they are!" she cries.

"Looking good!" Shandall says, handing me a cup of Gatorade.

"Thanks." I gulp the Gatorade and accept an energy gel.

"You're almost halfway," Linzy says. "You're doing great!"

We press on, and I squeeze the gel into my mouth a little at a time as I run.

It tastes like chocolate frosting, and it revives me a little. When I'm done, Gavin takes my empty pouch from me and asks, "You doing okay?"

I nod, but it's only halfhearted. "What's our pace?"

"Ten thirties at the four-mile mark."

"You're kidding."

He shakes his head.

"No wonder! I can't keep this up. It's killin' me!"

He immediately drops back the pace. "Hey!" he calls up to Fiona and Mario. "We've gotta ease up a little."

Fiona falls in beside me. "What's hurting?"

"I'm okay," I tell her. I keep my voice low so Rosa can't hear. "I've only run this weight five miles before, and it took me about an hour. That's, like, twelves, and we're doing ten thirties!"

Fiona slows down even more. "This better?"

I nod, but it's strange—it's like the damage is done, and slowing down isn't undoing it. My breathing won't fall into a comfortable rhythm, my hips have an unfamiliar ache to them, and my arms feel very heavy.

When we reach and crest the Queensland Drawbridge, I am immensely relieved.

"Halfway there!" Fiona says, pepping me along.

"And a bit of downhill," I say, grateful for gravity's help with the wheelchair.

The mile-six water stop is in the middle of nowhere—an oasis in a desert of dried grass. And what's even better than the oasis is that Annie and Giszelda are working the station.

"There they are!" Giszelda cries.

"Come 'n' get it, you crazy people!" Annie shouts.

"Crazy doesn't even begin to describe it! They're nuts!"

"Wackos!"

"A runnin' and rollin' insane asylum!"

"Amen!"

We all laugh and get our cups. I actually don't feel like drinking, but I hear Kyro's voice in my head: *Be smart—stay hydrated and keep your fuel up.*

So I drink.

And I take an energy gel.

And I press on.

Six miles, I tell myself. *Only four to go. One plus one plus one plus one.*

It feels a little fuzzy in my head. Like I've got the wrong number of ones. Like I'm so fatigued that I can't even count to four.

One plus one plus one plus one.

And somewhere in my fuzzy mind I make a connection—that's how everything is done.

One by one by one by one.

That's how I got through losing a leg.

Minute by minute by minute by minute.

Hour by hour by hour by hour.

Day by day by day by day.

That's how anybody makes it through anything.

So I dig in and decide that's how I'll face the miles ahead—one by one by one by one.

Something in that makes the pain easier to take, makes the effort easier to endure. And then, near the seven-mile mark, I realize we're passing by the cemetery.

I think about seeing Lucy's mom there the other morning.

I think about her making it through what had to be the hardest days of her life; how she had to take the minutes, the hours, the days, the months, one by one by one by one.

Suddenly I'm grateful that the ones I'm counting off are miles. Miles I'm *able* to run. Miles I asked for. Miles I've worked hard to face. My ones are a distance between me and victory, not days between me and tragedy.

Fiona's in step beside me, and I pant out, "Lucy," and nod up to the cemetery.

"Ohhhh," she says, and her face crinkles with sadness.

"We miss you, Lucy!" I call up the hill.

"We miss you, Lucy!" Fiona calls too.

All of us glance at one another, then together we shout, "WE MISS YOU, LUCY!"

The next stretch brings us back into neighborhoods. There aren't a lot of people out, but those who are, are loud and happy. Like the coffee has kicked in and the clapping is keeping them warm.

"GO, ROSA!" they shout, and then they realize that they've seen us on TV. "HEY—you're those girls! Good for you! You show 'em! GO, GO, GO!!"

Mario and Gavin start up with their clappers again, and Rosa waves and giggles and shouts, "THANK YOU!" to everyone who cheers for us, and keeps me going by calling to me over her shoulder, "This is the best day of my life!"

With each block the crowds get thicker.

People are out on their balconies getting an aerial view.

Rosa waves and clicks her clapper, but I'm slumping again. And my hips are killing me.

"Mile eight!" Gavin calls, pointing ahead.

Two to go, I tell myself. *One, and one more.*

I drink at the aid station, but only water. And although I try to eat the energy gel, I can't stomach it.

The crowds grow noisier, but I turn inward. I feel like I've hit the Rigor Mortis Bend of the River Run. It's only two more miles, but it's payback time for the two first miles—every step from here on is at a slight incline.

People are shouting my name, Rosa's name.

I see familiar faces.

I see my dad.

My mom.

Kaylee and her friends.

How did they get there?

I wave, I smile, but I don't really have the energy to do either.

Sounds are murky—they're having trouble making it through the pounding from inside.

I'm vaguely aware that we're passing people.

Runners who are now walking.

But we're being passed, too.

By men in grass skirts.

It's okay, I tell myself. *You're doing great. Run strong, run strong, run strong. . . .*

I don't even see the nine-mile marker as we go by. Gavin points it out. "Only one to go!" he calls, but it's like a ghost whispering in my ear.

My legs are lead.

My arms ache.

My hips are cramping, demanding I stop. Especially my left one. It's an agonizing knot of pain.

And my stump—it's hot.

Wet.

Angry.

Run strong, run strong, run strong. . . .

But I'm living step to step.

I start counting them.

I get to fifty and start over.

Step by step by step by step.

A young girl runs out from the crowd, touches me, and dashes away before I even know she's been there.

"GO, JESSICA!" I hear people shout.

"RO-SA! RO-SA! RO-SA!" they chant.

Then Fiona shouts, "There it is!"

I know what she means.

I look up; look out. There's a red-and-white balloon arch only fifty yards ahead.

"The finish line!" Rosa cries. "The finish line!"

I try to soak in the happy sounds of her voice, the ecstatic clacking of her clapper. I try to remember why I did this.

"RO-SA! RO-SA! RO-SA!"

"JES-SI-CA! JES-SI-CA!"

I dig in, dig deep. The cheering helps me find a hidden reserve.

The balloon arch is growing larger.

The crowd louder.

Larger.

Louder.

I manage a weak wave, a smile.

And then, with a *chirp-chirp-chirp-chirp*, we've crossed over.

Over the finish line.

I'm aware that people are taking pictures.

I'm aware that the news crew is there.

I'm aware that Rosa is in seventh heaven; that random strangers are talking to her and treating her like a friend. "It was great! Thank you!" she's telling them as a race-day helper cuts the timing chip off my shoe.

I'm aware that my family and Kyro are there, telling me how proud they are.

I'm aware that we're all making our way over to Regatta Park, where the breakfast celebration is being held.

It's all sort of fuzzy in my head because I'm shaky and exhausted, but I'm also aware that I'm very, very happy. I'm surrounded by friends, by family, by my teammates and coach, and by warm, supportive strangers. They've all helped me in some way get over that finish line.

But as we gather in Regatta Park and help ourselves to scrambled eggs, orange juice, and bagels, I realize something.

That wasn't a finish line for me.

Eight months ago it was a herculean effort to walk myself and my IV stand to the bathroom.

Today I ran my friend ten miles across her first finish line.

Eight months ago I couldn't do anything.

This race has made me believe that there's nothing I *can't* do.

This is my new starting line.

Acknowledgments

The following people were invaluable in helping me through this fascinating, educational, and extremely emotional journey:

Greg "Pegleg Greg" Birkholz, a true survivor who focuses on what he has, not what he's lost, and whose insider view and comments were very helpful.

Adele Schneidereit, who does indeed "inspire the world" with her accomplishments, her attitude, and her awareness campaign regarding cerebral palsy.

Greg "Sark" Sarkisian, track coach supreme and steadfast friend, who helped me fine-tune the track scenes.

John D. Hollingsead, CPO, whose cooperation and expertise were essential to the accuracy of this story.

Dana Cummings, executive director of the Association of Amputee Surfers, whose work with vets is amazing. I'll never forget our run through town.

Samantha Ford, whose cheerful spirit and love of dance are inspiring.

Mark Stipanov, whose background in prosthetics was extremely useful as I was struggling to climb the learning curve.

My high school track buddies, who faced the winds and forged strong spirits circling the Oval of Pain.

I would also like to thank:

My husband, Mark Parsons, for rooting me around the many hard curves of this book, and for always being there when I stumble . . . or need to go for a run.

My editor, Nancy Siscoe, who, after twenty-seven books together, still really works at helping me shape my stories. Her input is always constructive and astute.

My agent, Ginger Knowlton, for helping me get through Rigor Mortis Bend.

About the Author

Wendelin Van Draanen spent many years as a classroom teacher and is now a full-time writer. She is the author of many award-winning books, including the Sammy Keyes mysteries, *Flipped*, *Swear to Howdy*, *Runaway*, and *Confessions of a Serial Kisser*.

Ms. Van Draanen lives with her husband, two sons, and two dogs in California. Her hobbies include the "three R's": reading, running, and rock 'n' roll.

Wendelin Van Draanen and her husband are also the founders of Exercise the Right to Read, a nationwide campaign designed to get kids reading and running and to help schools raise funds for their libraries. Ms. Van Draanen ran her first marathon when the campaign kicked off, and seeing athletes with disabilities running strong provided much of the inspiration for this book.

To read more about Wendelin Van Draanen's books, please visit WendelinVanDraanen.com, and to learn more about Exercise the Right to Read, visit ExercisetheRight toRead.org.